Princess Tales

edited by Nora Kramer

Illustrated by Barbara Cooney

SCHOLASTIC BOOK SERVICES

NEW YORK · TORONTO · LONDON · AUCKLAND · SYDNEY · TOKYO

For reprint permission grateful acknowledgment is made to the following:

The Bobbs-Merrill Company, Inc., for "Ricky-of-the-Tuft" from FOLK TALES OF FRANCE, adapted by Polly Curren, © 1963 by The Bobbs-Merrill Company, Inc.

Criterion Books for "The Blackbird's Song" adapted from THE FAUN AND THE WOOD CUTTER'S DAUGHTER by Barbara Leonie Picard, © 1964 by Criterion Books, Inc.

John Farquharson Ltd., for "Melisande" by E. Nesbit.

Holt, Rinehart and Winston, Inc., for "The Handkerchief" adapted from THE SULTAN'S FOOL AND OTHER NORTH AFRICAN TALES by Robert Gilstrap and Irene Estabrook, © 1958 by Robert Gilstrap and Irene Estabrook; and "The Son of the Baker of Barra" from SEA-SPELL AND MOOR-MAGIC by Sorche Nic Leodhas, © 1968 by Leclaire G. Alger.

Little, Brown and Company for "The Twelve Dancing Princesses" from FAVORITE FAIRY TALES TOLD IN FRANCE by Virginia Haviland, text © 1959 by Virginia Haviland.

Parents' Magazine Press for THE PRACTICAL PRINCESS by Jay Williams, © 1969 by Jay Williams.

The Viking Press, Inc., for "The Princess and the Vagabone" from THE WAY OF THE STORYTELLER by Ruth Sawyer, copyright 1942, copyright © renewed 1970 by Ruth Sawyer.

ISBN: 0-590-09199-9

Copyright © 1971 by Scholastic Magazines, Inc. All rights reserved. Published by Scholastic Book Services, a division of Scholastic Magazines, Inc.

13 12 11 10 9 8 7 6 5 4 3   9/7 0 1 2 3 4/8

CONTENTS

The Practical Princess

Princess Bedelia was as lovely as the moon shining upon a lake full of water lilies. She was as graceful as a cat leaping. And she was also extremely practical.

When she was born, three fairies had come to her cradle to give her gifts as was usual in that country. The first fairy had given her beauty. The second had given her grace. But the third, who was a wise old creature, had said, "I give her common sense."

"I don't think much of that gift," said King Ludwig, raising his eyebrows. "What good is common sense to a princess? All she needs is charm."

Nevertheless, when Bedelia was eighteen years

old, something happened which made the king change his mind.

A dragon moved into the neighborhood. He settled in a dark cave on top of a mountain, and the first thing he did was to send a message to the king. "I must have a princess to devour," the message said, "or I shall breathe out my fiery breath and destroy the kingdom."

Sadly, King Ludwig called together his councilors and read them the message.

"Perhaps," said the prime minister, "we had better advertise for a knight to slay the dragon. That is what is generally done in these cases."

"I'm afraid we haven't time," answered the king. "The dragon has only given us until tomorrow morning. There is no help for it. We shall have to send him the princess."

Princess Bedelia had come to the meeting because, as she said, she liked to mind her own business and this was certainly her business.

"Rubbish!" she said. "Dragons can't tell the difference between princesses and anyone else. Use your common sense. He's just asking for me because he's a snob."

"That may be so," said her father, "but if we don't send you along, he'll destroy the kingdom."

"Right!" said Bedelia. "I see I'll have to deal with this myself." She left the council chamber. She got the largest and gaudiest of her state robes and stuffed it with straw, and tied it together with string. Into the center of the bundle she packed about a hundred pounds of gunpowder. She got two strong young men to carry it up the mountain for her. She stood in front of the dragon's cave and called, "Come out! Here's the princess!"

The dragon came blinking and peering out of the darkness. Seeing the bright robe covered with gold and silver embroidery, and hearing Bedelia's voice, he opened his mouth wide.

At once, at Bedelia's signal, the two young men swung the robe and gave it a good heave, right down the dragon's throat. Bedelia threw herself flat on the ground, and the two young men ran.

As the gunpowder met the flames inside the dragon, there was a tremendous explosion.

Bedelia got up, dusting herself off. "Dragons," she said, "are not very bright."

She left the two young men sweeping up the pieces, and she went back to the castle to have her geography lesson.

The lesson that morning was local geography.

"Our kingdom, Arapathia, is bounded on the north by Istven," said the teacher. "Lord Garp, the ruler of Istven, is old, crafty, rich, and greedy."

At that very moment, Lord Garp of Istven was arriving at the castle. Word of Bedelia's destruction of the dragon had reached him. "That girl," said he, "is just the wife for me." And he had come with a hundred finely dressed courtiers and many presents to ask King Ludwig for her hand.

The king sent for Bedelia. "My dear," he said, clearing his throat nervously, "just see who is here."

"I see. It's Lord Garp," said Bedelia. She turned to go.

"He wants to marry you," said the king.

Bedelia looked at Lord Garp. His face was like an old napkin, crumpled and wrinkled. It was covered with warts, as if someone had left crumbs on the napkin. He had only two teeth. Six long hairs grew from his chin, and none on his head. She felt like screaming.

However, she said, "I'm very flattered. Thank you, Lord Garp. Just let me talk to my father in private for a minute."

When they had retired to a small room behind the throne, Bedelia said to the king, "What will Lord Garp do if I refuse to marry him?"

"He is rich, greedy, and crafty," said the king, unhappily. "He is also used to having his own way in everything. He will be insulted. He will probably declare war on us, and then there will be trouble."

"Very well," said Bedelia. "We must be practical."

She returned to the throne room. Smiling sweetly

at Lord Garp, she said, "My lord, as you know, it is customary for a princess to set tasks for anyone who wishes to marry her. Surely you wouldn't like me to break the custom. And you are bold and powerful enough, I know, to perform any task."

"That is true," said Lord Garp smugly, stroking the six hairs on his chin. "Name your task."

"Bring me," said Bedelia, "a branch from the Jewel Tree of Paxis."

Lord Garp bowed, and off he went. "I think," said Bedelia to her father, "that we have seen the last of him. For Paxis is a thousand miles away, and the Jewel Tree is guarded by lions, serpents, and wolves."

But in two weeks, Lord Garp was back. With him he bore a chest, and from the chest he took a wonderful twig. Its bark was of rough gold. The leaves that grew from it were of fine silver. The twig was covered with blossoms, and each blossom had petals of mother-of-pearl and centers of sapphires, the color of the evening sky.

Bedelia's heart sank as she took the twig. But then she said to herself, "Use your common sense, my girl! Lord Garp never traveled two thousand miles in two weeks, nor is he the man to fight his way through lions, serpents, and wolves."

She looked more carefully at the branch. Then she said, "My lord, you know that the Jewel Tree of

Paxis is a living tree, although it is all made of jewels."

"Why, of course," said Lord Garp. "Everyone knows that."

"Well," said Bedelia, "then why is it that these blossoms have no scent?"

Lord Garp turned red.

"I think," Bedelia went on, "that this branch was made by the jewelers of Istven, who are the best in the world. Not very nice of you, my lord. Some people might even call it cheating."

Lord Garp shrugged. He was too old and rich to feel ashamed. But like many men used to having their own way, the more Bedelia refused him, the more he was determined to have her. "Never mind all that," he said. "Set me another task. This time, I swear I will perform it."

Bedelia sighed. "Very well. Then bring me a cloak made from the skins of the salamanders who live in the Volcano of Scoria."

Lord Garp bowed, and off he went. "The Volcano of Scoria," said Bedelia to her father, "is covered with red-hot lava. It burns steadily with great flames, and pours out poisonous smoke so that no one can come within a mile of it."

"You have certainly profited by your geography lessons," said the king, with admiration.

Nevertheless, in a week, Lord Garp was back. This time, he carried a cloak that shone and rippled with all the colors of fire. It was made of scaly skins, stitched together with fine golden wire. Each scale was red and orange and blue, like a tiny flame. Bedelia took the splendid cloak. She said to herself, "Use your head, miss! Lord Garp never climbed the red-hot slopes of the Volcano of Scoria."

A fire was burning in the fireplace of the throne room. Bedelia hurled the cloak into it. The skins blazed up in a flash, blackened, and fell to ashes.

Lord Garp's mouth fell open. Before he could speak, Bedelia said, "That cloak was a fake, my lord. The skins of salamanders who can live in the Volcano of Scoria wouldn't burn in a little fire like that one."

Lord Garp turned pale with anger. He hopped up and down, unable at first to do anything but splutter.

"Ub — ub — ub!" he cried. Then, controlling himself, he said, "So be it. If I can't have you, no one shall!"

He pointed a long, skinny finger at her. On the finger was a magic ring. At once, a great wind arose. It blew through the throne room. It sent King Ludwig flying one way and his guards the other. Bedelia was picked up and whisked off through the air. When she could catch her breath and look about her, she found herself in a room at the top of a tower.

Bedelia peered out of the window. About the

tower stretched an empty, barren plain. As she watched, a speck appeared in the distance. A plume of dust rose behind it. It drew nearer and became Lord Garp on horseback.

He rode to the tower and looked up at Bedelia. "Aha!" he croaked. "So you are safe and snug, are you? And will you marry me now?"

"Never," said Bedelia, firmly.

"Then stay there until never comes," snarled Lord Garp. Away he rode.

For the next two days, Bedelia felt very sorry for herself. She sat wistfully by the window, looking out at the empty plain. When she was hungry, food appeared on the table. When she was tired, she lay down on the narrow cot and slept. Each day Lord Garp rode by and asked if she had changed her mind, and each day she refused him. Her only hope was that, as so often happens in old tales, a prince might come riding by who would rescue her.

But on the third day, she gave herself a shake. "Now, then, pull yourself together," she said, sternly. "If you sit waiting for a prince to rescue you, you may sit here forever. Be practical! If there's any rescuing to be done, you're going to have to do it yourself."

She jumped up. There was something she had not yet done, and now she did it. She tried the door.

It opened.

Outside, were three other doors. But there was no

sign of a stair, or any way down from the top of the tower. She opened two of the doors and found that they led into cells just like hers, but empty. Behind the fourth door, however, lay what appeared to be a haystack. From beneath it came the sound of snores. And between snores, a voice said, "Six million and twelve . . . *snore* . . . six million and thirteen . . . *snore* . . . six million and fourteen . . ."

Cautiously, she went closer. Then she saw that what she had taken for a haystack was in fact an immense pile of blond hair. Parting it, she found a young man, sound asleep.

As she stared, he opened his eyes. He blinked at her. "Who — ?" he said. Then he said, "Six million and fifteen," closed his eyes, and fell asleep again.

Bedelia took him by the shoulder and shook him hard. He awoke, yawning, and tried to sit up. But the mass of hair made this difficult.

"What on earth is the matter with you?" Bedelia asked. "Who are you?"

"I am Prince Perian," he replied, "the rightful ruler of — oh, dear, here I go again. Six million and . . ." His eyes began to close.

Bedelia shook him again. He made a violent effort and managed to wake up enough to continue, " — of Istven. But Lord Garp has put me under a spell. I have to count sheep jumping over a fence, and this puts me to slee — ee — ee — " He began to snore lightly.

"Dear me," said Bedelia. "I must do something."

She thought hard. Then she pinched Perian's ear, and this woke him with a start.

"Listen," she said. "It's quite simple. It's all in your mind, you see. You are imagining the sheep jumping over the fence — No! Don't go to sleep again!

"This is what you must do. Imagine them jumping backwards. As you do, *count* them backwards, and when you get to *one*, you'll be wide awake."

The prince's eyes snapped open. "Marvelous!" he said. "Will it work?"

"It's bound to," said Bedelia. "If the sheep going one way will put you to sleep, their going back again will wake you up."

Hastily, the prince began to count, "Six million and fourteen, six million and thirteen, six million and twelve . . ."

"Oh, my goodness," cried Bedelia, "count by hundreds, or you'll never get there."

He began to gabble as fast as he could, and with each moment that passed, his eyes sparkled more brightly, his face grew livelier, and he seemed a little stronger, until at last he shouted, "Five, four, three, two, ONE!" and awoke completely.

He struggled to his feet, with a little help from Bedelia.

"Heavens!" he said. "Look how my hair and beard have grown. I've been here for years. Thank you, my dear. Who are you, and what are you doing here?"

Bedelia quickly explained.

Perian shook his head. "One more crime of Lord Garp's," he said. "We must escape and see that he is punished."

"Easier said than done," Bedelia replied. "There is no stair in this tower, as far as I can tell, and the outside wall is much too smooth to climb down."

Perian frowned. "This will take some thought," he said. "What we need is a long rope."

"Use your common sense," said Bedelia. "We haven't any rope."

Then her face lighted, and she clapped her hands. "But we have your beard," she laughed.

Perian understood at once, and chuckled. "I'm sure it will reach almost to the ground," he said. "But we haven't any scissors to cut it off with."

"That is so," said Bedelia. "Hang it out of the window and let me climb down. I'll search the tower and perhaps I can find a ladder, or a hidden stair. If all else fails, I can go for help."

She and the prince gathered up great armfuls of the beard and staggered into Bedelia's room, which had the largest window. The prince's long hair trailed behind and nearly tripped him. Perian threw the beard out of the window and braced himself, holding the beard with both hands to ease the pull

on his chin. Bedelia climbed out of the window and slid down the beard.

But suddenly, out of the wilderness came the drumming of hoofs, a cloud of dust, and then Lord Garp on his swift horse. With one glance, he saw what was happening. He shook his fist up at Prince Perian.

"Meddlesome fool!" he shouted. "I'll teach you to interfere."

He leaped from the horse and grabbed the beard. He gave it a tremendous yank. Headfirst came Perian, out of the window. Down he fell, and with a thump, he landed right on top of old Lord Garp.

This saved Perian, who was not hurt at all. But it was the end of Lord Garp.

Perian and Bedelia rode back to Istven on Lord Garp's horse.

In the great city, the prince was greeted with cheers of joy — once everyone had recognized him after so many years and under so much hair.

And of course, since Bedelia had rescued him from captivity, she married him. First, however, she made him get a haircut and a shave so that she could see what he really looked like. For she was always practical.

The Twelve
Dancing Princesses

ONCE UPON A TIME there lived in a small French
village a young cowherd named Michel, who had
no father or mother. As he was handsome, with blue
eyes and black hair, the village girls all admired
him. When he drove his cows to pasture, they often
called to him. But Michel would only go on without
looking at them. The truth is that he thought them
very homely. He had heard about beautiful princesses, and dreamed of marrying one of them.

One day, just at noon when the sun was hottest,
Michel ate his piece of dry bread for dinner and
went to sleep under an oak tree. He dreamed that a
beautiful lady, dressed in gold, came to him and

said, "Go to the castle of Beloeil and you shall marry a princess!"

That evening Michel told his dream to the farm people. They only made fun of him.

The next day at the same hour, Michel went to sleep again under the same tree. The lady appeared to him a second time, and said, "Go to the castle of Beloeil and you shall marry a princess!"

Again Michel told of his dream, and his friends laughed in his face. Never mind, he thought, if the lady should appear a third time, I will obey her.

The following day, about two o'clock in the afternoon, the little cowherd came down the road, singing as he drove his cows back early to the stable.

In a great rage, the farmer began to scold Michel, who only replied, "I am leaving."

Michel made his clothes into a bundle, said good-by, and set forth bravely. Through the valley, toward the castle of Beloeil, he trudged on. He wondered what lay ahead for him?

There was, indeed, something important.

It was known that in the castle of Beloeil lived twelve beautiful princesses. And they were as proud as they were beautiful, and so truly royal that they could feel a pea in their beds, even through ten mattresses.

It was known, too, that they lived like princesses,

and never rose until noon. Twelve beds they had, all in the same room. But what was most strange was that, though every night they were locked in by three bolts, every morning their satin shoes were worn out.

When asked what they did at night, the princesses always answered that they slept. No one ever heard any noise, and no one could understand how the shoes wore themselves out!

At last the Duke of Beloeil had his trumpeter announce that whoever could discover how his daughters wore out their shoes should choose one of the princesses for his wife.

On hearing this, a crowd of princes came to try their luck. They watched all night behind the open door of the princesses' room, but next morning the young men were gone, and no one could say what had become of them.

When Michel arrived at the castle, he went straight to the gardener and asked for work. The man had just dismissed his garden boy, so, although Michel did not look like a very strong boy, the gardener hired him. He thought the boy's good looks would please the princesses.

Michel's first duty, when the princesses arose, was to give each one a bouquet. He placed himself behind their door, with twelve bouquets in a basket.

The princesses took them without even looking at him — except Lina, the youngest, who admired him with her dark, velvety eyes.

Michel knew that all the princes had disappeared while trying to learn the secret of the shoes. But Princess Lina's beautiful eyes gave him a great desire to try, himself.

Michel now had a new dream. The lady in gold came to him again, holding in one hand two young trees, a cherry laurel and a rose laurel. In her other hand she held a little golden rake, a little golden pail, and a silken towel.

She said to him, "Plant these little trees in two large pots, rake them with the rake, water them with the pail, and dry them with the towel. When they have grown as tall as a girl of fifteen, say to each of them, 'My beautiful laurel, with the golden rake I have raked you, with the golden pail I have watered you, with the silken towel I have dried you.' Ask then for whatever you wish, and the laurels will give it to you."

Michel thanked the lady. When he awoke from his dream he found the two laurels beside him. Carefully he obeyed the lady's orders.

The trees grew fast. When they were as tall as a girl of fifteen, Michel said to the cherry laurel, "My lovely cherry laurel, with the golden rake I have raked you, with the golden pail I have watered you, with the silken towel I have dried you. . . . Show me how to become invisible."

That evening, when the princesses went to bed, Michel followed them, barefoot, and hid under one of the twelve beds.

The princesses set to work opening cupboards and boxes. They put on the most beautiful dresses, and turned all around to admire themselves in their mirrors. From his hiding place Michel could see nothing, but he could hear the princesses skipping about and laughing.

At last the eldest said, "Be quick, girls; our dancing partners will be waiting."

When Michel dared peep out, he saw the twelve sisters splendidly dressed, with satin shoes on their feet, and in their hands the bouquets he had brought them.

"Are you ready?" asked the eldest.

"Yes," replied the other eleven, and took their places in line behind her.

The eldest princess clapped her hands three times and a trap door opened. They all disappeared down a hidden staircase, and Michel hastened to follow. As he was walking close to Princess Lina, he carelessly stepped on her dress.

"There is someone behind me," cried the princess, "holding onto my dress!"

"Stupid!" said her eldest sister. "You are always

afraid of something. Some nail has caught your dress."

Down, down, down they went. At last they came through a passage to a door closed by only a latch. The eldest princess opened it. They went out into a beautiful wood, where the leaves were spangled with drops of silver. Beyond that was another wood, where the leaves were sprinkled with gold. From there they went through a third, where the leaves were strewn with diamonds.

Michel saw next a large lake. On its shore awaited twelve little rowboats, decorated with flags. In each one sat a prince, grasping the oars. Each princess entered a boat, and Michel slipped in with Princess Lina.

The boats moved along rapidly. But Lina's, being heavier, lagged behind.

"We don't go so quickly as usual," said the princess. "What can be the reason?"

"I don't know," answered the prince. "I'm rowing as hard as I can."

Ahead lay a fine castle, splendidly lighted. From it sounded lively music. In a moment the boats landed. The princes gave their arms to the princesses, and they all entered the castle.

Michel followed them into the ballroom. The sight dazzled him — the mirrors, the lights, the flowers, and the rich hangings. Hiding in a corner, he admired the grace and beauty of the princesses as they danced. He thought Lina, with her velvety eyes, the most beautiful and lovable. And how eagerly she danced! It was plain that she loved dancing better than anything else.

Poor Michel envied those handsome young men with whom Lina danced so gracefully. But he did not know how little reason he had to be jealous.

These young men were really the princes who had tried to learn the princesses' secret. The princesses had given each of them a drink, to enchant them into forgetting everything but the love of dancing.

Everyone danced on till the shoes of the princesses were full of holes. After a supper of the princesses' favorite dishes, they went back to their boats.

Again they crossed the wood with the diamond-strewn leaves, the wood with the gold-sprinkled leaves, and the wood whose leaves were spangled with drops of silver. For proof of what he had seen, Michel broke off a small silver branch. Lina turned around at the noise it made.

"What was that noise?" she asked.

"It was nothing," replied her eldest sister. "It was only the screech of the owl at the castle."

Back at the castle, Michel slipped ahead and ran up the staircase, reaching the princesses' room ahead of them. He opened the window and slid down a vine into the garden. Just as the sky was becoming light, he set to work.

That day, when Michel made up the bouquets, he hid the branch spangled with silver drops in the flowers for the little princess. When Lina discovered it, she was much surprised. However, she said nothing about it.

In the evening, the twelve sisters went again to the ball. Michel followed and crossed the lake in Lina's boat. This time the prince complained that the boat seemed heavy.

"It is the heat," replied the princess. "I, too, have been feeling very warm."

During the ball, she looked everywhere for the garden boy, but in vain.

As they came back, Michel gathered a branch from the wood with the gold-sprinkled leaves. Now it was the eldest princess who heard the noise it made in breaking.

"It's nothing," said Lina — "only the cry of the owl."

The next morning, Lina found the gold-sprinkled branch in her bouquet. This time she asked the garden boy, "Where does this come from?"

"Your Royal Highness knows well enough," answered Michel.

"So you have followed us?"

"Yes, princess."

"How did you manage it? We never saw you."

"I hid," replied Michel.

The princess was silent a moment. Then she said, "You know our secret — be sure to keep it!" She threw down a bag of gold pieces. "Here is something to keep you quiet." But Michel only walked away without picking it up.

For three nights Lina neither saw nor heard anything unusual. On the fourth, however, she heard a noise in the wood with diamond-strewn leaves. The next noon there was a branch from it in her bouquet.

She took Michel aside and said to him crossly, "You know what my father has promised to pay for our secret?"

"Yes, I know, princess."

"Don't you mean to sell it to him?"

"No."

"Are you afraid?"

"No, princess."

"What makes you keep quiet about it?"

Michel was silent.

Lina's sisters had seen her talking to the garden boy and made fun of her.

"What keeps you from marrying him?" asked the eldest. "You would become a gardener too. It is a pretty profession. You could live in the cottage at the end of the park, and help your husband draw water from the well. When we get up in the morning, you could bring us our bouquets."

Then Princess Lina became very angry. When Michel gave her a bouquet, she accepted it coldly.

Michel was most respectful and never raised his eyes to her. Yet nearly all day she felt him at her side without ever seeing him.

One afternoon Lina decided to tell everything to her eldest sister.

"What!" said that one. "This rogue knows our secret and you waited this long to tell me! I shall get rid of him at once."

"But how?"

"Why, by having him taken to the tower with the dungeons."

Lina and the eldest sister decided to discuss this with the other ten sisters. All agreed with the eldest that Michel should go to the tower.

Then Lina declared that if they touched a hair of the garden boy she would go and tell their father the secret of the holes in their shoes!

So instead it was arranged that Michel should go to the ball. At the end of supper he would take the drink, which would enchant him like the others.

Now Michel had been present, invisible, when the princesses talked about this. He had made up his mind to take the drink. He would sacrifice himself thus for the happiness of the one he loved.

But, in order to look well at the ball, he now went

to the laurels and said: "My lovely rose laurel, with the golden rake I have raked you, with the golden pail I have watered you, with the silken towel I have dried you. . . . Dress me like a prince."

A beautiful pink flower appeared. Michel picked it. In a moment he found himself clothed in velvet as black as the eyes of the little princess. The blossom of the rose laurel adorned his jacket.

Thus dressed, he went that evening to the Duke of Beloeil. The duke gave him leave to try to discover his daughters' secret. Michel looked so fine that no one recognized him as the garden boy.

The twelve princesses went upstairs to bed. Michel followed. He hid behind the open door, waiting for the signal to leave. This time he did not cross in Lina's boat. He gave his arm to the eldest sister.

During the evening, Michel danced with each in turn. He moved so gracefully that everyone was delighted with him. At last, the time came for him to dance with the little princess. She found him the best partner in the world, but he dared not speak a single word to her.

When the satin slippers were worn through, the fiddles stopped. The dancers all sat down at the banquet table. Michel was placed next to the eldest sister and opposite Lina.

The sisters gave Michel the most delicious food and drink, and the most flattering compliments.

At last, the eldest sister made a sign. One of the pages brought in a large golden cup.

Michel threw a last look at the little princess. He accepted the cup and lifted it to his lips.

"Don't drink!" Lina suddenly cried. "I would *rather* be a gardener's wife!"

Michel at once flung the contents of the cup behind him. He sprang over the table and fell at Lina's feet.

The other princes then fell likewise at the knees of the princesses. Each chose a husband and raised him to her side. The charm was broken!

The twelve couples entered the boats, which had to cross back many times in order to carry over the other princes. They all went through the enchanted groves. When they had passed through the underground door, they heard a great noise, as if the fairy castle were tumbling down.

They went straight to the Duke of Beloeil, who had just awakened. Michel held forth the golden cup and revealed the secret of the holes in the shoes.

"Choose, then," said the duke, "whichever princess you prefer."

"My choice is already made," replied Michel. He held out his hand to the youngest princess.

But the Princess Lina did not become a gardener's wife. Instead, Michel became a prince!

The Princess
and the Vagabone

In the golden time, when an Irish king sat in
every province and plenty filled the land, there
lived in Connaught a grand old king with one
daughter. She was as tall and slender as the reeds,
and her face was the fairest in seven counties. This
was more the pity, for the temper she had did not
match it at all, at all — it was the ugliest that ever
fell to the birthlot of a princess. She was proud, she
was haughty, and her tongue had the sharpness of
thorns. From the day she was born till long after she
was a woman grown she was never heard to say a
kind word or known to do a kind deed to a living
creature.

As each year passed, the king would think to himself, " 'Tis the New Year will see her better." But it was worse instead of better she grew, until one day the king found himself at the end of his patience.

"Faith, another man shall have her for the next eighteen years, for, by my soul, I've had my fill of her!"

So it came about, as I am telling ye, that the king sent word to the nobles of the neighboring provinces that whosoever would win the consent of his daughter in marriage should have half of his kingdom and the whole of his blessing.

On the day that she was eighteen they came — a wonderful procession of earls, dukes, princes, and kings, riding up to the castle gate, acourting. The air was filled with the ring of the silver trappings on their horses, and the courtyard was gay with the colors of banners and the long cloaks they wore. The king made each welcome according to his rank; and then he sent a servingman to his daughter, bidding her come and choose her suitor, the time being ripe for her to marry. It was a courteous message that the king sent, but the princess heard little of it. She flew into the hall on the heels of the servingman, like a fowl-hawk after a bantam cock. Her eyes burned with the anger that was hot in her heart, while she stamped her foot in the king's face until the rafters rang with the noise of it.

"So, ye will be giving me away for the asking —
to any one of these blithering fools who has a rag to
his back or a castle to his name?"

The king grew crimsom at her words. He was
ashamed that they should all hear how sharp was
her tongue. Moreover, he was fearsome lest they
should take to their heels and leave him with a
shrew on his hands for another eighteen years. He
was hard at work piecing together a speech when
the princess strode past him on to the first suitor in
the line.

"At any rate, I'll not be choosing ye, ye long-
legged corncrake," and she gave him a sound kick
as she went on to the next — a large man with a
shaggy beard. Seeing how the first suitor had fared,
he tried a wee bit of a smile on her while his hand
went out coaxingly. She saw, and her anger grew
threefold. She sprang at him, digging her hands
deep in his beard, and then she wagged his foolish
head back and forth, screaming, "Take that, and
that, and that, ye old whiskered rascal!"

It was a miracle that any beard was left on his
face the way that she pulled it. But she let him go
free at last, and turned to a thin, sharp-faced prince
with a monstrous long nose. The nose took her
fancy, and she gave it a tweak, telling the prince to
take himself home before he did any damage with
it. The next one she called "pudding face" and

slapped his fat cheeks until they were purple, and the poor lad groaned with the sting of it.

"Go back to your trough, for I'll not marry a grunter!" said she.

She moved swiftly down the line in less time than it takes for the telling. It came to the mind of many of the suitors that they would be doing a wise thing if they betook themselves off before their turn came. So as many of them as were not fastened to the floor with fear started away. There happened to be one prince just making for the door when the princess looked around. In a trice she reached out for the tongs that stood on the hearth near by, and she laid it across his shoulders, sending him spinning into the yard.

"Take that, ye old gander, and good riddance to ye!" she cried after him.

It was then that she saw looking at her a great towering giant of a man, and his eyes burned through hers, deep down into her soul. So great was he that he could have picked her up with a single hand and thrown her after the gander, and she knew it yet she felt no fear. He was as handsome as Nuada of the Silver Hand: and not a mortal fault could she have found with him, not if she had tried for a hundred years. The two of them stood facing each other, glaring, as if each would spring at the other's throat the next moment. But all the while, the princess was thinking, and thinking how wonderful he was, from the top of his curling black hair, down the seven feet of him, to the golden clasps on his shoes.

What the man was thinking I cannot be telling. Like a breath of wind on a smoldering fire her liking for him set her anger fierce-burning again. She gave him a sound cuff on the ear, then turned, and with a sob in her throat she went flying from the room, the servingmen scattering before her as if she had been a hundred million robbers on a raid.

And the king? Faith, he was dumb with rage. But when he saw the blow that his daughter had given to the finest gentleman in all of Ireland, he went after her as if he had been two hundred million constables on the trail of robbers.

"Ye are a disgrace and a shame to me," said he, catching up with her and holding firmly to her two hands. "And, what's more, ye are a disgrace and a blemish to my castle and my kingdom. I'll not keep ye in it a day longer. The first traveling vagabone who comes begging at the door shall have ye for his wife."

"Will he?" and the princess tossed her head in the king's face and went to her chamber.

The next morning a poor wandering singer came to the castle to sell a song for a penny or a morsel of bread. The song was sweet that he sang, and as

Oona, the lady-in-waiting wound strands of her mistress's long black hair with golden thread, the princess listened.

> "The gay young wren sang over the moor.
> 'I'll build me a nest,' sang he.
> ' 'Twill have a thatch and a wee latched door,
> For the wind blows cold from the sea.
> And I'll let no one but my true love in,
> For she is the mate for me.'
> Sang the gay young wren.
>
> The wee brown wren by the hedgerow cried,
> 'I'll wait for him here,' cried she.
> 'For the way is far and the world is wide,
> And he might miss the way to me.
> Long is the time when the heart is shut,
> But I'll open to none save he,'
> Sang the wee brown wren."

A strange throb came to the heart of the princess when the song was done. She pulled her hair free from Oona's hands.

"Get silver," she said; "I would throw it to him." And when she saw the wonderment grow in Oona's face, she added: "The song pleased me. Can I not pay for what I like without having ye look at me as if ye feared my wits had flown? Go, get the silver!"

But when she pushed open the grating and leaned far out to throw it, the singer had gone.

For the king had heard the song as well as the princess. His rage was still with him, and when he saw who it was, he lost no time, but called him quickly inside.

"Ye are as fine a vagabone as I could wish for," he said. "Maybe ye are not knowing it, but ye are a bridegroom this day." And the king went on to tell him the whole tale. The tale being finished, he sent ten strong men to bring the princess down.

A king's word was law in those days. The vagabone knew this — and, what's more, he knew he must marry the princess, whether he liked it or no. The vagabone had great height, but he stooped so that it shortened the length of him. His hair was long, and it fell, uncombed and matted, about his shoulders. His brogues were patched, and his hose were sadly worn, and with his rags, he was the sorriest cut of a man that a maid ever laid her two eyes on. When the princess came, she was dressed in a gown of gold, with jewels hanging from every thread of it, and her cap was caught with a jeweled brooch. She looked as beautiful as a May morning — with a thundercloud rising back of the hills. The vagabone held his breath for a moment, watching her. Then he pulled the king gently by the arm.

"I'll not have a wife that looks grander than myself. If I marry your daughter, I must marry her in rags — the same as my own."

The king agreed 'twas a good idea, and sent for the worst dress of rags in the whole countryside. The rags were fetched, the princess dressed, the priest brought, and the two of them married; and, though she cried and she kicked and she cuffed and she prayed, she was the vagabone's wife — hard and fast.

"Now take her, and good luck go with ye," said the king. Then his eyes fell on the tongs by the hearth. "Here, take these along — they may come in handy on the road."

Out of the castle gate, across the gardens, and into the country that lay beyond went the princess and the vagabone. The sky was blue over their heads and the air was full of spring. Each wee creature that passed them on the road seemed bursting with the joy of it. There was naught but anger in the princess's heart, however — and what was in the heart of the vagabone I cannot be telling. This I know, that he sang the "Song of the Wren" as they went. Often and often the princess turned back on the road or sat down swearing she would go no farther. And often and often did she feel the weight of the tongs across her shoulders that day.

At noon the two sat down by the crossroads to rest.

"I am hungry," said the princess. "Not a morsel of food have I tasted this day. Ye will go get me some."

"Not I, my dear," said the vagabone; "ye will go beg for yourself."

"Never," said the princess.

"Then ye'll go hungry," said the vagabone. And that was all. He lighted his pipe and went to sleep with one eye open and the tongs under him.

One, two, three hours passed, and the sun hung low in the sky. The princess sat there until hunger drove her to her feet. She rose wearily and stumbled to the road and as she reached it a great coach drawn by six black horses came galloping up. The princess made a sign for it to stop. Though she was in rags, yet she was still so beautiful that the coachman drew in the horses and asked her what she was wanting.

"I am near to starving," and as she spoke the tears started to her eyes, while a new soft note crept into her voice. "Do ye think your master could spare me a bit of food — or a shilling?" and the hand that had been used to strike went out for the first time to beg.

It was a prince who rode inside the coach that day, and he heard her. Reaching out a fine, big hamper through the window, he told her she was hearty welcome to whatever she found in it, along with his blessing. But as she put up her arms for it, she saw that the prince was none other than the fat suitor whose face she had slapped on the day before. Then anger came back to her again for the shame of begging from him. She emptied the hamper — chicken pasty, jam currant bread, and all — on top of his head, peering through the window, and threw the empty basket at the coachman. Away drove the coach. Away ran the princess, and threw herself, sobbing, on the ground near the vagabone.

" 'Twas a good dinner that ye lost," said the vagabone; and that was all.

That night they reached a wee scrap of a cabin on the side of a hill. The vagabone climbed the steps and opened the door. "Here we are at home, my dear," said he.

"What kind of a home do ye call this?" and the princess stamped her foot. "Faith, I'll not live in it."

"Then ye can live outside; it's all the same to me." The vagabone went in and closed the door after him, and in a moment he was whistling merrily the song of the wee brown wren.

The princess sat down on the ground and nursed her poor tired knees. She had walked many a mile that day, with a heavy heart and an empty stomach — two of the worst traveling companions ye can find. The night came down, black as a raven's wing, and the dew fell, heavy as rain, wetting the rags and chilling the princess to the marrow. The wind blew fresh from the sea, and the wolves began their howling in the woods near by. And at last, what with the cold and the fear and the loneliness of it, she could bear it no longer, and she crept softly up to the cabin and went in.

"There's the creepy stool by the fire, waiting for ye," said the vagabone — and that was all. But late in the night he lifted her from the chimney corner where she had dropped asleep and laid her gently on the bed, which was freshly made and clean. And he sat by the hearth till dawn, keeping the fuel piled high on the fire, so that cold could not waken her. Once he left the hearth. Coming to the bedside, he stood a moment to watch her while she slept, and he stooped and kissed the wee pink palm of her hand that lay there like a half-closed water lily.

Next morning the first thing the Princess asked was where was the breakfast, and where were the servants to wait on her, and where were some decent clothes.

"Your servants are your own two hands, and they will serve ye well when ye teach them how," was the answer she got.

"I'll have neither breakfast nor clothes if I have to be getting them myself. And shame on ye for treating a wife so," and the princess caught up a wooden pail and threw it at the vagabone.

He jumped clear of it, and it struck the wall behind him. "Have your own way, my dear," and he left her, to go out on the bogs and cut turf for fuel.

That night the princess hung the kettle and made stir-about and griddle bread for the two of them.

" 'Tis the best I have tasted since I was a lad and my mother made the baking," said the vagabone, and that was all. But often and often his lips touched the braids of her hair as she passed him in the dark. And again he sat through the night, keeping the fire and mending her wee leather shoes, that they might be whole the next day.

Next day he brought some twigs and showed her how to weave them into creels to sell on coming marketday. But the twigs cut her fingers until they bled, and the princess cried, making the vagabone white with rage. Never had she seen such a rage in another creature. He threw the twigs about the cabin, making them whirl and eddy like leaves before an autumn wind. He stamped upon the half-made creel, crushing it to pulp under his feet. Catching up the table, he tore it to splinters, throwing the fragments into the fire, where they blazed.

"By Saint Patrick, 'tis a bad bargain that ye are! I will take ye this day to the castle in the next county, where I hear they are needing a scullery maid. And there I'll apprentice ye to the king's cook."

"I will not go," said the princess. But even as she spoke fear showed in her eyes and her knees began shaking in under her.

"Aye, but ye will, my dear," and the vagabone took up the tongs quietly from the hearth.

For a month the princess worked in the castle of the king, and all that time she never saw the vagabone. Often and often she said to herself fiercely that she was well rid of him; but often, as she sat alone after her work in the cool of the night, she would wish for the song of the wee brown wren, while a new loneliness crept deeper and deeper into her heart.

She worked hard about the kitchen, and as she scrubbed the pots and turned the spit and cleaned the floor with fresh white sand she listened to the wonderful tales the other servants had to tell of the king. They had it that he was the handsomest, strongest, king in all of Ireland, and every man and child and little creature in his kingdom worshiped him. And after the tales were told the princess would say to herself, "If I had not been so proud and free with my tongue, I might have married such a king, and ruled his kingdom with him, learning kindness."

Now it happened one day that the princess was told to be unusually spry and careful about her work. There was a monstrous deal of it to be done — cakes to be iced and puddings to be boiled, fat ducks to be roasted, and a whole suckling pig put on the spit to turn.

"What's the meaning of all this?" asked the princess.

The cook looked at her pityingly. "Haven't you

heard the king is to be married this day to the fairest princess in seven counties?"

"Once that was I," thought the princess, and she sighed.

"What makes ye sigh?" asked the cook.

"I was wishing, just, that I could be having a peep at her and the king."

"Faith, that's possible. Do your work well, and maybe I can put ye where ye can see without being seen."

So it came about, as I am telling ye, at the end of the day, when the feast was ready and the guests come, that the princess was hidden behind the curtains in the great hall. There, where no one could see her, she watched the hundreds upon hundreds of fair ladies and fine noblemen in their silken dresses and shining coats, all silver and gold, march back and forth across the hall, laughing and talking and making merry among themselves. Then the pipers began to play, and everybody was still. From the farthest end of the hall came two and twenty lads in white and gold. These were followed by two and twenty pipers in green and gold and two and twenty bowmen in saffron and gold, and, last of all, the king.

A scream, a wee wisp of a cry, broke from the princess, and she would have fallen had she not caught one of the curtains. For the king was as tall and strong and beautiful as Nuada of the Silver

Hand. And from the top of his curling black hair down the seven feet of him to the golden clasps of his shoes he was every whit as handsome as he had been that day when she had cuffed him in her father's castle.

The king heard the cry and stopped the pipers. "I think," said he, "there's a scullery maid behind the curtains. Someone fetch her to me."

A hundred hands pulled the princess out. A hundred more pushed her across the hall to the feet of the king, and held her there, fearing lest she escape. "What were ye doing there?" the king asked.

"Looking at ye, and wishing I had the undoing of things I have done," and the princess hung her head and sobbed piteously.

"Nay, sweetheart, things are best as they are," and there came a look into the king's eyes that blinded those watching, so that they turned away and left the two alone.

"Heart of mine," he went on, softly, "are ye not knowing me?"

"Ye are putting more shame on me because of my evil tongue and the blow my hand gave ye that day."

"Faith, it is not so. Look at me."

Slowly the eyes of the princess looked into the eyes of the king. For a moment she could not be reading them. She was as a child who pores over a strange tale after light fades and it has grown too dark to see. But bit by bit the meaning of it came to her, and her heart grew glad with the wonder of it. Out went her arms to him with the cry of loneliness that had been hers so long.

"I never dreamed that it was ye, never once."

"Can ye ever love and forgive?" asked the king.

"Hush ye!" and the princess laid her finger on his lips.

The ladies-in-waiting were called and she was led away. Her rags were changed for a dress that was spun from gold and woven with pearls, and her beauty shone about her like a great light. They were married again that night, for none of the guests were knowing of that first wedding long ago.

Late o' that night a singer came under the Princess's window, and very softly the words of his song came to her:

"The gay young wren sang over the moor.
'I'll build me a nest,' sang he.
' 'Twill have a thatch and a wee latched door,
For the wind blows cold from the sea.
And I'll let no one but my true love in,
For she is the mate for me,'
Sang the gay young wren.

The wee brown wren by the hedgerow cried,
'I'll wait for him here,' cried she.
'For the way is far and the world is wide,

And he might miss the way to me.
Long is the time when the heart is shut,
But I'll open to none save he,'
Sang the wee brown wren."

The grating opened slowly. The princess leaned
far out, her eyes like stars in the night, and when
she spoke there was naught but gentleness and love
in her voice.

"Here is the silver I would have thrown ye on a
day long gone by. Shall I throw it now, or will ye
come for it?"

And that was how a princess of Connaught was
won by a king who was a vagabone.

Melisande

WHEN THE Princess Melisande was born, her mother, the queen, wished to have a christening party, but the king put his foot down and said he would not have it.

"I've seen too much trouble come of christening parties," said he. "However carefully you keep your visiting book, some fairy or other is sure to get left out, and you know what *that* leads to. Why, even in my own family the most shocking things have occurred. The Fairy Malevola was not asked to my great-grandmother's christening — and you know all about the spindle and the hundred years' sleep."

"Perhaps you're right," said the queen. "My own

cousin by marriage forgot some stuffy old fairy or other when she was sending out the cards for her daughter's christening, and the old wretch turned up at the last moment, and the girl drops toads out of her mouth to this day."

"Just so. And there was that business of the mouse and the kitchenmaids," said the king. "We'll have no nonsense about it. I'll be her godfather, and you shall be her godmother, and we won't ask a single fairy — then none of them can be offended."

"Unless they all are," said the queen.

And that was exactly what happened. When the king and queen and the baby got back from the christening, the parlormaid met them at the door, and said, "Please, Your Majesty, several ladies have called. I told them you were not at home, but they all said they'd wait."

"Are they in the parlor?" asked the queen.

"I've shown them into the throne room, Your Majesty," said the parlormaid. "You see, there are several of them."

There were about seven hundred. The great throne room was crammed with fairies, of all ages and of all degrees of beauty and ugliness — good fairies and bad fairies, flower fairies and moon fairies, fairies like spiders and fairies like butterflies — and as the queen opened the door and began to say how sorry she was to have kept them waiting, they all cried, with one voice: "Why didn't you ask *me* to your christening party?"

"I haven't had a party," said the queen, and she turned to the king and whispered, "I told you so." This was her only consolation.

"You've had a christening," said the fairies, all together.

"I'm very sorry," said the poor queen, but Malevola pushed forward and said, "Hold your tongue!" most rudely.

Malevola is the oldest, as well as the most wicked, of the fairies. She is deservedly unpopular, and has been left out of more christening parties than all the rest of the fairies put together.

"Don't begin to make excuses," she said, shaking her finger at the queen. "That only makes your conduct worse. You know well enough what happens if a fairy is left out of a christening party. We are all going to give our christening presents *now*. As the fairy of highest social position, I shall begin. The princess shall be bald."

The queen nearly fainted as Malevola drew back and another fairy, in a smart bonnet with snakes in it, stepped forward with a rustle of bats' wings. But the king stepped forward too.

"No, you don't!" said he. "I wonder at you, ladies, I do indeed. How can you be so unfairylike? Have none of you been to school — have none of you studied the history of your own race? Surely you don't need a poor, ignorant king like me to tell you that this is *no go?*"

"How dare you?" cried the fairy in the bonnet, and the snakes in it quivered as she tossed her head. "It is my turn, and I say the princess shall be — "

The king actually put his hand over her mouth.

"Look here," he said, "I won't have it. Listen to reason — or you'll be sorry afterward. A fairy who breaks the traditions of fairy history goes out — you know she does — like the flame of a candle. And all tradition shows that only *one* bad fairy is ever forgotten at a christening party and the good ones are always invited. So either this is not a christening party or else you were all invited except one, and, by her own showing, that was Malevola. It nearly always is. Do I make myself clear?"

Several of the better-class fairies who had been led away by Malevola's influence murmured that there was something in what His Majesty said.

"Try it, if you don't believe me," said the king. "Give your nasty gifts to my innocent child — but as sure as you do, out you go, like a candle flame. Now, then, will you risk it?"

No one answered, and presently several fairies came up to the queen and said what a pleasant party it had been, but they really must be going. This example decided the rest. One by one all the fairies

said good-by and thanked the queen for the delight-
ful afternoon they had spent with her.

"It's been quite too lovely," said the lady with the
snake bonnet. "Do ask us again soon, dear queen. I
shall be so *longing* to see you again, and the *dear*
baby," and off she went, with the snake trimming
quivering more than ever.

When the very last fairy was gone, the queen ran
to look at the baby — she tore off its lace cap and
burst into tears. For all the baby's downy golden
hair came off with the cap, and the Princess Melisande was as bald as an egg.

"Don't cry, my love," said the king. "I have a wish
lying by, which I've never had occasion to use. My
fairy godmother gave it me for a wedding present,
but since then I've had nothing to wish for!"

"Thank you, dear," said the queen, smiling
through her tears.

"I'll keep the wish till baby grows up," the king
went on. "And then I'll give it to her, and if she likes
to wish for hair, she can."

"Oh, won't you wish for it *now?*" said the queen,
dropping mixed tears and kisses on the baby's
round, smooth head.

"No, dearest. She may want something else more
when she grows up. And, besides, her hair may
grow by itself."

But it never did. Princess Melisande grew up as

beautiful as the sun and as good as gold, but never a hair grew on that little head of hers. The queen sewed her little caps of green silk, and the princess's pink and white face looked out of these like a flower peeping out of its bud. And every day as she grew older she grew dearer, and as she grew dearer she grew better, and as she grew more good she grew more beautiful.

Now, when she was grown up, the queen said to the king:

"My love, our dear daughter is old enough to know what she wants. Let her have the wish."

So the king wrote to his fairy godmother and sent the letter by a butterfly. He asked if he might hand on to his daughter the wish the fairy had given him for a wedding present.

"I have never had occasion to use it," said he, "though it has always made me happy to remember that I had such a thing in the house. The wish is as good as new, and my daughter is now of an age to appreciate so valuable a present."

To which the fairy replied by return of butterfly:

Dear King,

Pray do whatever you like with my poor little present. I had quite forgotten it, but I am pleased to think that you have treasured my humble keepsake all these years.

Your affectionate godmother,
FORTUNA F.

So the king unlocked his gold safe with the several diamond-handled keys that hung at his girdle, and took out the wish and gave it to his daughter.

And Melisande said: "Father, I will wish all your subjects should be quite happy."

But they were that already, because the king and queen were so good. So the wish did not go off.

So then she said, "Then I wish them all to be good."

But they were that already, because they were happy. So again the wish hung fire.

Then the queen said, "Dearest, for my sake, wish what I tell you."

"Why, of course I will," said Melisande. The queen whispered in her ear, and Melisande nodded. Then she said aloud, "I wish I had golden hair a yard long, and that it would grow an inch every day, and grow twice as fast every time it was cut, and — "

"Stop," cried the king. And the wish went off, and the next moment the princess stood smiling at him through a shower of golden hair.

"Oh, how lovely," said the queen. "What a pity you interrupted her, dear. She hadn't finished."

"What was the end?" asked the king.

"Oh," said Melisande, "I was only going to say, 'and twice as thick.'"

"It's a very good thing you didn't," said the king. "You've done about enough." For he had a mathematical mind and could do the sums about the grains of wheat on the chessboard, and the nails in the horse's shoes, in his royal head without any trouble at all.

"Why, what's the matter?" asked the queen.

"You'll know soon enough," said the king. "Come, let's be happy while we may. Give me a kiss, little Melisande, and then go to Nurse and ask her to teach you how to comb your hair."

"I know," said Melisande, "I've often combed Mother's."

"Your mother has beautiful hair," said the king, "but I fancy you will find your own less easy to manage."

And, indeed, it was so. The princess's hair began by being a yard long, and it grew an inch every night. If you know anything at all about the simplest sums, you will see that in about five weeks her hair was about two yards long. This is a very inconvenient length. It trails on the floor and sweeps up all the dust, and though in palaces, of course, it is all gold dust, still it is not nice to have it in your hair. And the princess's hair was growing an inch every night. When it was three yards long, the princess could not bear it any longer — it was so heavy and so hot — so she borrowed Nurse's cutting-out scissors and cut it all off, and then for a few hours she was confortable. But the hair went on growing, and now it grew twice as fast as before — so that in thirty-six days it was as long as ever. The poor princess cried with tiredness; when she couldn't bear it any more, she cut her hair and was comfortable for a very little time. For the hair now grew four times as fast as at first, and in eighteen days it was as long as before and she had to have it cut. Then it grew eight inches a day, and the next time it was cut it grew sixteen inches a day, and then thirty-two inches and sixty-four and a hundred and twenty-eight inches a day, and so on, growing twice as fast after each cutting, till the princess would go to bed at night with her hair clipped short, and wake up in the morning with yards and yards and yards of golden hair flowing all about the room, so that she could not move without pulling her own hair, and Nurse had to come and cut the hair off before she could get out of bed.

"I wish I was bald again," sighed poor Melisande, looking at the little green caps she used to wear, and she cried herself to sleep o' nights between the golden billows of the golden hair. But she never let her mother see her cry, because it was the queen's fault, and Melisande did not want to seem to reproach her.

When first the princess's hair grew, her mother sent locks of it to all her royal relations, who had them set in rings and brooches. Later the queen was able to send enough for bracelets and belts. But

presently so much hair was cut off that they had to burn it. Then when autumn came all the crops failed. It seemed as though all the gold of harvest had gone into the princess's hair. And there was a famine.

Then Melisande said, "It seems a pity to waste all my hair; it does grow so very fast. Couldn't we stuff things with it, or something, and sell them to feed the people?"

So the king called a council of merchants, and they sent out samples of the princess's hair, and soon orders came pouring in. Soon the princess's hair became the staple export of that country. They stuffed pillows with it, and they stuffed beds with it. They made ropes of it for sailors to use, and curtains for hanging in king's palaces. They made haircloth of it, for hermits and other people who wished to be uncomfy. But it was so soft and silky that it only made them happy and warm, which they did not wish to be. So the hermits gave up wearing it, and, instead, mothers bought it for their little babies, and all well-born infants wore little shirts of princess haircloth.

And still the hair grew and grew. And the people were fed and the famine came to an end.

Then the king said, "It was all very well while the famine lasted — but now I shall write to my fairy godmother and see if something cannot be done."

So he wrote and sent the letter by a skylark, and by return of bird came this answer:

"Why not advertise for a competent prince? Offer the usual reward."

So the king sent out his heralds all over the world to proclaim that any respectable prince with proper references should marry the princess Melisande if he could stop her hair growing.

Then from far and near came trains of princes anxious to try their luck, and they brought all sorts of nasty things with them in bottles and round wooden boxes. The princess tried all the remedies, but she did not like any of the princes, so in her heart she was rather glad that none of the nasty things in bottles and boxes made the least difference to her hair.

The princess had to sleep in the great throne room now, because no other room was big enough to hold her and her hair. When she woke in the morning the long room would be quite full of her golden hair, packed tight and thick like wool in a barn. And every night when she had had the hair cut close to her head she would sit in her green silk gown by the window and cry, and kiss the little green caps she used to wear, and wish herself bald again.

It was as she sat crying there on Midsummer Eve that she first saw Prince Florizel.

He had come to the palace that evening, but he would not appear in her presence with the dust of travel on him, and she had retired with her hair borne by twenty pages before he had bathed and changed his garments and entered the reception room.

Now he was walking in the garden in the moonlight, and he looked up and she looked down, and for the first time Melisande, looking on a prince, wished that he might have the power to stop her hair from growing. As for the prince, he wished many things, and the first was granted him. For he said, "You are Melisande?"

"And you are Florizel?"

"There are many roses round your window," said he to her, "and none down here."

She threw him one of three white roses she held in her hand. Then he said, "White rose trees are strong. May I climb up to you?"

"Surely," said the princess.

So he climbed up to the window.

"Now," said he, "if I can do what your father asks, will you marry me?"

"My father has promised that I shall," said Melisande, playing with the white roses in her hand.

"Dear princess," said he, "your father's promise is nothing to me. I want yours. Will you give it to me?"

"Yes," said she, and gave him the second rose.

"I want your hand."

"Yes," she said.

"And your heart with it."

"Yes," said the princess, and she gave him the third rose.

"And a kiss to seal the promise."

"Yes," said she.

"And a kiss to go with the hand."

"Yes," she said.

"And a kiss to bring the heart."

"Yes," said the princess, and she gave him the three kisses.

"Now," said he, when he had given them back to her, "tonight do not go to bed. Stay by your window, and I will stay down here in the garden and watch. And when your hair has grown to the filling of your room, call to me, and then do as I tell you."

"I will," said the princess.

So at dewy sunrise the prince, lying on the turf beside the sundial, heard her voice.

"Florizel! Florizel! My hair has grown so long that it is pushing me out of the window."

"Get out onto the window sill," said he, "and twist your hair three times round the great iron hook that is there."

And she did.

Then the prince climbed up the rose bush with

his naked sword in his teeth, and he took the Princess's hair in his hand about a yard from her head and said, "Jump!"

The princess jumped, and screamed, for there she was hanging from the hook by a yard and a half of her bright hair. The prince tightened his grasp of the hair and drew his sword across it.

Then he let her down gently by her hair till her feet were on the grass, and jumped down after her.

They stayed talking in the garden till all the shadows had crept under their proper trees and the sundial said it was breakfast time.

Then they went in to breakfast, and all the court crowded round to wonder and admire. For the princess's hair had not grown.

"How did you do it?" asked the king, shaking Florizel warmly by the hand.

"The simplest thing in the world," said Florizel modestly. "You have always cut the hair off the princess. I just cut the princess off the hair."

"Humph!" said the king, who had a logical mind. And during breakfast he more than once looked anxiously at his daughter. When they got up from breakfast the princess rose with the rest, but she rose and rose and rose, till it seemed as though there would never be an end of it. The princess was nine feet high.

"I feared as much," said the king sadly. "I wonder

what will be the rate of progression. You see," he said to poor Florizel, "when we cut the hair off, *it* grows — when we cut the princess off, *she* grows. I wish you had happened to think of that!"

The princess went on growing. By dinner time she was so large that she had to have her dinner brought out into the garden because she was too large to get indoors. But she was too unhappy to be able to eat anything. And she cried so much that there was quite a pool in the garden, and several pages were nearly drowned. So she remembered her *Alice in Wonderland* and stopped crying at once. But she did not stop growing. She grew bigger and bigger and bigger, till she had to go outside the palace gardens and sit on the common, and even that was too small to hold her comfortably, for every hour she grew twice as much as she had done the hour before. And nobody knew what to do, nor where the princess was to sleep. Fortunately, her clothes had grown with her, or she would have been very cold indeed, and now she sat on the common in her green gown, embroidered with gold, looking like a great hill covered with gorse in flower.

You cannot possibly imagine how large the princess was growing, and her mother stood wringing her hands on the castle tower, and the Prince Florizel looked on brokenhearted to see his princess snatched from his arms and turned into a lady as big as a mountain.

The king did not weep or look on. He sat down at once and wrote to his fairy godmother, asking her advice. He sent a weasel with the letter, and by return of weasel he got his own letter back again, marked "Gone away. Left no address."

It was now, when the kingdom was plunged into gloom, that a neighboring king took it into his head to send an invading army against the island where Melisande lived. They came in ships and they landed in great numbers, and Melisande, looking down from her height, saw alien soldiers marching on the sacred soil of her country.

"I don't mind so much now," said she, "if I can really be of some use this size."

And she picked up the army of the enemy in handfuls and double handfuls, and put them back in their ships, and gave a little flip to each transport ship with her finger and thumb, which sent the ships off so fast that they never stopped till they reached their own country, and when they arrived there the whole army to a man said it would rather be court-martialed a hundred times over than go near the place again.

Meanwhile Melisande, sitting on the highest hill on the island, felt the land trembling and shivering under her giant feet.

"I do believe I'm getting too heavy," she said, and jumped off the island into the sea, which was just up to her ankles. Just then a great fleet of warships and gunboats and torpedo boats came in sight, on their way to attack the island.

Melisande could easily have sunk them all with one kick, but she did not like to do this because it might have drowned the sailors, and, besides, it might have swamped the island.

So she simply stooped and picked the island as you would pick a mushroom — for, of course, all islands are supported by a stalk underneath — and carried it away to another part of the world. So that when the warships got to where the island was marked on the map, they found nothing but sea, and a very rough sea it was, because the princess had churned it all up with her ankles as she walked away through it with the island.

When Melisande reached a suitable place, very sunny and warm, and with no sharks in the water, she set down the island. And the people made it fast with anchors, and then everyone went to bed, thanking the kind fate which had sent them so great a princess to help them in their need, and calling her the savior of her country and the bulwark of the nation.

But it is poor work being the nation's bulwark and your country's savior when you are miles high, and have no one to talk to, and when all you want is to be your humble right size again and to marry your sweetheart. And when it was dark the princess came close to the island, and looked down, from far up, at her palace and her tower, and cried and cried and cried. It does not matter how much you cry into the sea, it hardly makes any difference, however large you may be. Then when everything was quite dark the princess looked up at the stars.

"I wonder how soon I shall be big enough to knock my head against them," said she.

And as she stood star-gazing she heard a whisper right in her ear. A very little whisper, but quite plain.

"Cut off your hair!" it said.

Now, everything the princess was wearing had grown big along with her, so that now there dangled from her golden belt a pair of scissors as big as the Malay Peninsula, together with a pincushion the size of the Isle of Wight and a yard measure that would have gone round Australia.

And when she heard the little, little voice, she knew it, small as it was, for the dear voice of Prince Florizel, and she whipped out the scissors from her gold case and snip, snip, snipped all her hair off, and it fell into the sea. The coral insects got hold of it at once and set to work on it, and now they have made it into the biggest coral reef in the world; but that has nothing to do with the story.

Then the voice said, "Get close to the island," and the princess did, but she could not get very close because she was so large, and she looked up again at the stars and they seemed to be much farther off.

Then the voice said, "Be ready to swim," and she felt something climb out of her ear and clamber down her arm. The stars got farther and farther away, and next moment the princess found herself swimming in the sea, and Prince Florizel swimming beside her.

"I crept onto your hand when you were carrying the island," he explained, when their feet touched the sand and they walked in through the shallow water, "and I got into your ear with an ear trumpet. You never noticed me because you were so great then."

"Oh, my dear prince," cried Melisande, falling into his arms, "you have saved me. I am my proper size again."

So they went home and told the king and queen. Both were very, very happy, but the king rubbed his chin with his hand and said:

"You've certainly had some fun for your money, young man, but don't you see that we're just where we were before? Why, the child's hair is growing already."

And indeed it was.

Then once more the king sent a letter to his godmother. He sent it by a flying fish, and by return of fish came the answer:

"Just back from my holidays. Sorry for your troubles. Why not try scales?"

And on this message the whole court pondered for weeks.

But the prince caused a pair of gold scales to be made, and hung them in the palace gardens under a big oak tree. And one morning he said to the princess, "My darling Melisande, I must really speak seriously to you. We are getting on in life. I am nearly twenty: it is time that we thought of being settled. Will you trust me entirely and get into one of those gold scales?"

So he took her down into the garden and helped her into the scale, and she curled up in it in her green and gold gown, like a little grass mound with buttercups on it.

"And what is going into the other scale?" asked Melisande.

"Your hair," said Florizel. "You see, when your hair is cut off you, it grows, and when you are cut off your hair, you grow — oh, my heart's delight, I can never forget how you grow, never! But if, when your hair is no more than you, and you are no more than your hair, I snip the scissors between you and it, then neither you nor your hair can possibly decide which ought to go on growing."

"Suppose *both* did," said the poor princess humbly.

"Impossible," said the prince, with a shudder. "There are limits even to Malevola's malevolence. And, besides, Fortuna said, 'Scales.' " Will you try it?"

"I will do whatever you wish," said the poor princess. "But let me kiss my father and mother once, and Nurse, and you too, my dear, in case I grow large again and can kiss nobody any more."

So they came one by one and kissed the princess.

Then the nurse cut off the princess's hair, and at once it began to grow at a frightful rate.

The king and queen and nurse busily packed it, as it grew, into the other scale, and gradually the scale went down a little. The prince stood waiting between the scales with his drawn sword, and just before the two were equal he struck. But during the time his sword took to flash through the air the princess's hair grew a yard or two, so that at the instant when he struck, the balance was true.

"You are a young man of sound judgment," said the king, embracing him, while the queen and the nurse ran to help the princess out of the gold scale.

The scale full of golden hair bumped down onto the ground as the princess stepped out of the other one and stood there before those who loved her, laughing and crying with happiness, because she remained her proper size, and her hair was not growing any more.

She kissed her prince a hundred times, and the very next day they were married. Everyone remarked on the beauty of the bride, and it was noticed that her hair was quite short — only five feet five and a quarter inches long — just down to her pretty ankles. Because the scales had been ten feet ten and a half inches apart, and the Prince, having a straight eye, had cut the golden hair exactly in the middle!

The Handkerchief

THERE WAS ONCE a lovely and clever young Arabian princess who lived with her father, the Grand Vizier of Morocco. Her name was Zakia (Zah-KEE-ah), and although she was only eighteen years old, she was so wise that her father rarely made a decision without first asking his daughter's advice.

One day, however, he made a decision without consulting Zakia, and it displeased her very much. The sultan, who was the absolute ruler of Morocco, had asked the grand vizier for Zakia's hand in marriage, and Zakia's father had consented to the union.

"No, Father," Zakia said firmly, when her father

told her about it. "I will not marry a man merely because you say so. I do not love him, and I refuse even to consider marrying him."

"But Zakia," he begged, "no girl would refuse a proposal of marriage from the sultan. The very idea of what might happen to me makes me shudder when I think of it. If you do not marry him, I may lose my head. Oh, please do as I say, my daughter. Marry him for my sake, I beg you."

The pleadings of her father finally moved Zakia to consent to the marriage — but only on one condition.

"The sultan must learn a trade, father," she demanded. "I will marry him only if he does so. What would happen to us if one day he lost his throne? Soon we would be penniless, and with no way to earn a living, we would starve to death."

Zakia's father was afraid that his daughter's demand would anger the sultan greatly. But even so, it was better than saying that Zakia had refused to become the sultan's bride.

When the sultan heard Zakia's request, he was pleased. And his pleasure greatly surprised Zakia's father who had trembled as he told of his daughter's demand.

"Your daughter is more than beautiful and talented," the sultan said royally. "She is also more clever than I had guessed. I will be glad to do as she asks, for I know our life together will be happy."

As soon as Zakia's father left the throne room, the sultan commanded that workers from all trades assemble before him and tell him about their occupations. After listening to each description the sultan thought carefully about what had been said. Then he made his decision.

"I shall become a weaver," he declared, in a pleased voice. "Out of all the trades I could study, I feel that I would enjoy this more than any other. Let me begin at once to learn the weaver's art so that I may fulfill the request of my beloved Zakia, and thus make our marriage a reality."

Soon the sultan was arising much earlier than usual each morning, and after completing official business, he departed for a room in a far corner of the palace. The room contained a loom, shuttles, and yarn, and soon after he entered it, the sound of his work could be heard by all who passed by. The sultan was a serious and sincere man.

As time went on, the sultan realized that he had indeed made a wise decision in becoming a weaver. Not only did he enjoy his work very much, but he discovered he had much natural talent along these lines. Satisfied with his progress, he began to weave a beautiful handkerchief to send to Zakia as proof of his weaving ability.

With loving care the sultan created an exquisite silken handkerchief. The center design was an embroidered red rose set against a forest background.

"Take this to Zakia, daughter of the grand vizier," the sultan commanded a servant, "and tell her that if this meets with her approval, our marriage shall take place within the month." And so the messenger did as the sultan ordered.

When Zakia opened her gift and saw the beautiful handkerchief, she was delighted. It was proof of the sultan's love for her, and soon they were married.

After the festive wedding, the young couple ruled the people of Morocco fairly and justly. Zakia's wise advice proved so helpful to the sultan in handling his affairs, that each day he grew more pleased he had chosen Zakia for his wife.

On one particular day when the sultan was much troubled with a problem, he came to his wife for counsel.

"How can I become more understanding of the common people of my country?" the sultan asked his wife. "How can I learn to think as they think, know their problems, and be aware of their needs?"

Zakia thought for a moment and then said in her soft voice, "My lord, it has been said by those far wiser than I, that if a man wishes to know another man he must live with him. Thus I feel that if you are to know the common people better, you must live among the common people. Why do you not disguise yourself as a common man, and go out to meet the people you rule?"

Zakia's suggestion pleased her husband. So, during the following week the sultan, his chamberlain, and one of his viziers walked the streets of Morocco wearing ragged dirty robes.

"I feel that this idea of Zakia's is most worthwhile," the sultan commented to his friends. "I feel I already know better the lives of my subjects and their needs."

"You are right, my lord," the chamberlain said. "But now can we not return to the palace to eat? I am starved."

"Why go back to the palace?" the sultan asked. "We are trying to find out more about the common people of Morocco, are we not?"

His companions nodded their heads in agreement.

"Would we not learn more if we were to eat in one of the restaurants where my subjects eat?" the sultan suggested to his hungry companions.

Agreeing that this indeed would be wise, the three men chose a small café that seemed hospitable.

"This looks like a fine place," the sultan commented. "And I must admit, my hunger grows with each passing minute."

The three men approached the café, but as they stepped on the threshold, they felt the floor slip away beneath them. Before they realized quite what had happened they found themselves in a deep, dark, underground pit. And although the men shouted, no one came to help them.

"A wonderful welcome for the sultan," the vizier complained angrily. "I wonder where we could be and what is expected of us."

"We are in a deep, dark hole," the sultan answered seriously. "But why are we here? Surely we have not been recognized in our ragged clothing. And even if we had been, who would want to harm us?"

Since the other two could give no answers to the sultan's questions, there was silence.

Suddenly a strange, high laugh echoed through the dark pit. The laugh was followed by the glimmering of a small candle, and above the candle was a face, dark and wrinkled.

"Say your prayers, you miserable ones," the holder of the candle screeched. "You are here to be fattened like cattle. In three days our butcher will slaughter you, and you will be served in our café which is famed for its excellent food."

"Have mercy, man," the chamberlain cried. "We came here for food. We are starving. Must you torture us this way?"

The wrinkled man laughed even louder, then disappeared into the darkness.

"Let us tell him who we are when he returns," the vizier said earnestly. "Then when they release us, we can arrest them and put a stop to their vile business."

"You are foolish, my vizier," the sultan answered. "If they should find out that I am the sultan, they would kill us quicker than ever. The fear of the people's anger will force them to destroy us without delay."

"You are right, my lord," the chamberlain agreed. "The vizier in his fright was thinking too hastily. But what do you suggest?"

"If only Zakia were here," the sultan said thoughtfully. "She would find a way out of this predicament, I know. But give me time to think."

The three men groped in the darkness to find the wall of the dungeon, and then they sat down against it to rest and think.

Hours later the jailer returned.

"Noble lord," the sultan said gently, "we did not intend to be impudent nor to displease you. We have learned what is to be our fate, and have resigned ourselves, for we know that our death is your desire. However, before we die please allow us to make a proposition. It could fill your pockets with gold, and at the same time, perhaps, spare our miserable lives."

"Your talk sounds very interesting," he said. "Continue."

"I am a weaver by trade," the sultan told him. "In fact, my work is so highly valued at the court of the sultan that the ladies of the harem will pay large prices for my handiwork. Give me a loom and some silken yarn, and by selling my products you will be able to make a considerable fortune. And as for us, we would much rather spend the rest of our lives weaving for you than be eaten in the café above."

The jailer's eyes gleamed as he listened, and without hesitation decided to accept the proposal.

Within the hour, a loom had been brought to the dungeon and the sultan started weaving a silken handkerchief similar to the one that he had woven for Zakia.

He worked feverishly by lamplight through the long hours of the night and when he had completed the handkerchief, he gave it to the jailer, saying, "Take this immediately to the sultan's wife, Zakia, in the sultan's palace. Surely she will buy the handkerchief and pay you well."

When the jailer reached the palace he found everything in a state of confusion. Messengers ran in and out of the throne room and guards gathered to form a search party to seek the missing sultan.

Unnoticed, the jailer slipped through the crowd of people, and up to Zakia, who was trying her best to keep back the tears and hide the grief that had filled her heart since her husband's disappearance.

"My mistress," the jailer said, "here I have a handkerchief woven by a famous weaver of Morocco. Would you like to buy it?"

When Zakia saw the handkerchief she recognized immediately the design, and knew without a doubt that the sultan had sent it as a message.

"Yes, it is a beautiful handkerchief," she said in an effort not to show her excitement. "I will buy it."

Then she gave the jailer the money, sent him on his way, and signaled quickly to two of the guards to follow him.

When the guards reached the café they heard the voices of the sultan, the vizier, and the chamberlain. Immediately one of them returned to summon the troops of the palace.

Silently the guards encircled the small stone building. As Zakia herself watched from her black stallion, the guards crept into the café. Then there was the sound of violent fighting.

When all was silent again, out of the café came the sultan borne on the shoulders of his soldiers. The vizier and the chamberlain followed behind.

"My darling Zakia," the sultan cried when he saw his wife waiting for him. "My life again is made more wonderful by your presence and cleverness. I owe my life to the one I love more dearly than anything else in the world."

Zakia was happy to hear her husband's words. And as she rode back to the palace alongside the handsome sultan, she realized for the first time how happy she was to be the wife of such a clever and talented man.

The Blackbird's Song

Many years ago there lived a young artist named Benedict. He had come to the city to study painting and he soon showed great promise and skill. In a few years his work surpassed that of all the other painters of the city.

Benedict quickly became rich and bought himself a fine house with large gardens, where he lived surrounded by beautiful things and the work of other artists.

Many people at the king's court bought his pictures, and he painted the portraits of some of them. His fame spread until at last the king himself learned of his skill and thought it would be a fine thing to have his portrait painted by this young man. It would hang in the palace and be a reminder to posterity of his royalty and greatness when he was long dead. So the king sent for Benedict and commanded him to paint his picture.

Now the king was not the type of person whom Benedict liked to paint. He was hard and cruel and mean and Benedict liked people to be happy and kind, with smiling faces and smiling hearts. But because he was the king, the young artist could not refuse, so he said, "I am honored, Your Majesty," and prepared to begin on the work.

Every day for an hour Benedict went to the palace and painted the king sitting on his gilded throne, wearing his crown and his ceremonial robes; and at the end of a month the portrait was done. Benedict always painted things as they really were. So he had painted the king looking hard and cruel and mean — to have done anything else would have been to betray his art, and he could not bring himself to do that.

When the king saw the portrait he was very angry, but he could say little without admitting that Benedict had seen and painted him truly. So giving no reason, he had Benedict thrown into prison, and the painting burned.

The young painter was left in a dungeon under the palace. It was cold and always twilight there, since the only light came through a narrow slit with two bars set high up in the wall. He was quite alone, without even a rat or a spider for company. He saw only the jailer once a day when he unlocked the door to give him his food. At first Benedict had tried to be friendly but he never received a word in reply — not even "Good morning."

Hour after hour he would sit on the narrow bench that served as a bed, with his head in his hands, remembering how it had been in the old days, when he had seen the sun and heard voices and laughter. He thought of his house and the beautiful things it held; and his friends, the feasts they had had, the music, the dancing — and the memories hurt.

But the greatest pain of all was when he remembered his work. He thought of the paintings he had done and the many more he had hoped to do. He longed for a brush and a palette, even though there was so little light to use them by. In his dungeon the days passed like years, while outside in the world life went on as it had always done.

In the palace, the king's daughter, the Princess Isabella, celebrated her sixteenth birthday and was allowed for the first time to take part in the life of the court. The princess was beautiful, and unlike her father — being gentle and kind and loving — like her mother the queen, who had died many years before. She loved flowers and birds, and she kept a blackbird in a golden cage. The door of the cage was always open so that it could fly away. But it had grown fond of the princess and her gentle voice and it would perch on her finger and let her hold it in her hands, and it never flew far from her.

Every afternoon the Princess Isabella walked in the palace gardens, watching the flowers as they opened in the sun, or picking a rose for her hair. Often her blackbird would be with her, singing to her from a tree or a wall as she walked, and she would call it to her and it would fly down and rest on her finger.

One day it alighted on the sill of the tiny window of the dungeon where Benedict lay and began to sing. It was the first bird he had heard since he had finished his portrait of the king. It sang to him of the sunlight and the green trees outside; the gardens with flowers that opened in the warmth, and the butterflies flitting among them. The young painter listened and tried hard not to weep. When the song was over the blackbird flew away. But it came again the next afternoon and sang of the fields where the buttercups bloomed, and the hawthorn hedges sugared with blossom. And on each day after that it came and brought comfort to him with its songs of the world outside.

One day, when its song was done, it slipped through the bars and flew down into the dungeon and fluttered around for a moment before flying out and away again. Benedict saved a crust for it, and the next time it came the blackbird, who ate little cakes off a princess's plate, deigned to share the stale bread that was all a prisoner had to offer. It pecked up the crumbs in the dim dungeon light. After that it flew down often to Benedict, and when it had finished its song, sometimes it would perch on his hand. The days seemed less lonely and less hopeless for Benedict now that he had a friend.

One day, from outside the window, it sang to him of the beauty of the Princess Isabella; her kind heart and her sweet low voice, her soft dark hair and her deep blue eyes, her lips like rose petals which could smile so sweetly, and the delicate blush of her cheek. Benedict listened entranced. When the song was over, he thought, "If only I might paint her." All that night he lay awake thinking, "If I had my paints and my brushes with me I could do such work as I have never done before."

For three days after he thought of nothing else, and the next day he could keep silent no longer. When the jailer came to bring food Benedict begged him to fetch him a brush and some paints and something to paint upon. The jailer refused. Benedict twisted the last gold button off his jacket. "This is all I have to give you," he said. "Take it and do as I ask, I beg of you."

The jailer thought how he could have taken the

button without earning it at any time during the past months, had he wanted it, and he said in his mind, "What a fool he is." And he took the button without a word and went.

But the next morning when he silently handed Benedict his bread and a pitcher of water, there was something wrapped in a dirty cloth tied to the loaf. When the young artist opened it he found it contained a paintbrush, a little paint, and a scrap of parchment rolled up and fastened with a thread. He could hardly believe his luck, and settled down at once to think out how he should begin his painting. The brush was a poor one, the few paints the wrong colors, and there was so little light in the dungeon that it was only at midday when the sun was highest that he could see well enough to paint at all. But he was not a great artist for nothing, and slowly the work was done. When it was completed, Benedict knew that he had never made anything finer. He had painted the princess as the blackbird had sung her to be, and so true was the likeness, it was as though she had been there with him each day for him to copy every feature of her lovely face.

When next the blackbird flew down into the dungeon, Benedict rolled up the parchment carefully and tied it with a hair. "Take this to the princess for me," he pleaded. And the blackbird flew with the parchment in its beak and alighted on the finger of

the Princess Isabella, where she walked in the garden among the roses. "What have you brought me, my friend?" she asked, and unrolled the parchment.

When she saw her portrait her joy was great. She showed it to her ladies and every one of them agreed that it was a perfect likeness. When the king heard of the picture, he demanded to see it. As soon as he set eyes on it he knew that such exquisite work could only have been done by one man. But he knew, too, that Benedict could not have seen the Princess Isabella, for she had taken no part in the life of the court before he had been imprisoned. The king could not understand how he could have painted her as she was without once having met her.

He said nothing to the princess of his thoughts, but only asked that he might keep the picture by him a few hours. Then he sent for Benedict to be brought to him. When the young artist had been led up the dark winding corridors from the dungeon, the king held out the parchment. "Have you seen this before?" he asked.

"Not by so good a light as I am seeing it now, Your Majesty," said Benedict with a smile.

"You do not deny that you painted it?"

"Why should I deny it? The work is good, I am not ashamed of it."

"Where did you see the princess?" demanded the king.

"I have never seen her," replied Benedict.

"There is witchcraft in this," said the king. "You are in league with a witch."

"That is untrue," said Benedict. "What would a witch have to do with one so beautiful and good as the princess?"

"Where did the paints and this parchment come from?" asked the king. And when Benedict was silent he repeated his question.

And because the young painter did not want to betray the jailer's kindness, he laughed a little and said, "Perhaps the witch brought me those."

"You are guilty of witchcraft," said the king. "You have confessed." And all those in the room looked at each other with startled eyes. "There is only one penalty for witchcraft," the king went on. "Tomorrow morning you die."

"Dying can be no worse than living alone in the darkness," thought Benedict. "And at least, when they take me out tomorrow to burn or to hang, I shall see the sky and the trees once again. And if fate is kind to me, the sun will be shining."

"That is all," said the king. "Take the prisoner away."

"Your Majesty," asked Benedict, "if I am to die tomorrow, will you grant me one last request?"

The king would have refused, but there were two ambassadors present from another land and he did

not want them to carry home a report of his mean-
ness to one who had but a few hours to live. So he
said, "As long as you do not ask for your life or a
delay in carrying out the sentence, I will grant your
request."

"Let me see the Princess Isabella, and speak with
her, for but two minutes before I die."

The king was very angry, but he had given his
word and he could not refuse. So he sent a message
to the princess that a young man who had been con-
demned to die on the following day wished as his
last request to see her before his death.

The princess was playing chess when the message
was brought to her. "The poor young man," she
said, and her eyes filled with tears. "What a strange
request. I must go at once."

She was wearing pink silk with silver and pearls,
so she took off her jewels and sent for a dress of
black velvet, for she did not want to appear too gay
in the presence of a man who was about to die. But
when she looked at herself in the mirror, in black
with a grey veil over her hair, she thought, "What
does it matter whether it is fitting for the occasion or
not? He has never seen me before and he will never
see me again; let him see me at my best." And she
carefully chose her loveliest ball dress of blue and
gold brocade, and put on her finest jewels as though

she were going to a dance, and wore a golden crown with diamonds upon her soft dark hair.

When, glittering and resplendent, she swept into the room where she was awaited, the courtiers whispered, "She has never looked more beautiful than today." And the two ambassadors from other lands murmured to one another, "We have no ladies so beautiful at home."

And Benedict saw her and thought with joy, "She is just as I knew she was," and he loved her with all his heart. Then he said quietly, "It was kind of you to come, Your Highness. I am glad to have seen you before I die, and to know that you are just as I painted you."

"Was it you, then, who painted my picture?"

"It was I," he said — and she no longer looked at him as at a stranger about to die. She saw instead someone who knew her so well that he could paint her perfect likeness before he even met her — and she knew that she would love him all her life.

"You must not die," she said in a low voice.

He shook his head and smiled a little. "There is no help for it." He knelt to kiss her hand. "I shall die the happier for having seen you."

"The two minutes are ended," said the king. "Take the prisoner away."

"You must not die," the princess whispered. "I love you."

But the guards took Benedict back to the dungeon, and when he was alone again he thought, "It is wonderful that she loves me, but had I known what was going to happen, I should never have asked to see her. I would not have her grieve for my death."

The princess begged her father to spare the young artist's life, but he would not listen to her or heed her tears. Later, when her ladies tried to cheer her, she sent them away. "I would rather be alone with my blackbird," she said. "Perhaps he will sing and comfort me." But the cage was empty. The blackbird was nowhere to be found, and all that night it did not return.

In the morning the guards came for Benedict and led him out of the palace and through the streets to the marketplace where he was to die. Fate had been kind to him and the sun was shining, with not a single cloud to spoil the blue sky.

But when they came to the marketplace, a tiny black cloud appeared over the sun. "If it is going to rain," thought Benedict, "it might have waited till I was dead. Though I suppose I should not be ungrateful that even the sky sheds a few tears for me."

The cloud came nearer, and became larger and darker the nearer it came. When its shadow lay over the city, people began to grow afraid. But they need have feared nothing, for the cloud was only all the singing birds in the world called together by the princess's blackbird. Over the city they divided into two clouds. One cloud went to the palace and the other to the marketplace, where with a fluttering of thousands of wings it descended and enveloped the young painter, rose in the air again, and bore him away.

In her room the princess heard a tapping on the pane and looked up. "It is my blackbird," she said, and ran to open the window.

Below the window she saw a cloud of birds and knew at once what she must do. Before anyone could stop her she had climbed on to the window sill and jumped. The birds surrounded her as she fell and bore her up in their midst. Then they rose high in the air and joined with the other cloud of birds above the marketplace.

The birds carried the Princess Isabella and the young painter far away into another land where the king could not find them. Here Benedict and the princess were married and lived in great contentment. And because Benedict was a very great artist they were soon rich again. They had a beautiful house with a wide garden — and in that garden, summer and winter alike, singing birds in their hundreds might always be heard.

Ricky-of-the-Tuft

MANY YEARS AGO a homely child was born to a queen. The poor queen was heartbroken when she saw her small, ugly son.

Only one fairy had been present at the birth of this baby, and when she saw the sadness of her queen, she tried to console her.

"Don't be sad, Queen," she said. "I will give your son a gift. He will be more intelligent and far wittier than any other man in the world. And he will be able to give this gift to the one he loves the most."

The queen felt better when she heard this. "If my son cannot be handsome, I am glad he will be brilliant," she said, with a smile.

Because the baby had an odd tuft of hair growing on his small head, she named him Ricky-of-the-Tuft.

As soon as he was able to talk, Ricky began to say a thousand clever and witty things. He was so gay and lively that everyone was charmed by him.

Seven or eight years later, two little girls were born to the queen of the neighboring country. The first little girl was a beautiful baby and the queen was very proud. "There has never been such a lovely child — anywhere!" she boasted joyfully.

The same fairy that had been at the birth of Ricky-of-the-Tuft was at this birth too. She was afraid that the queen was growing too proud and boastful. "Your daughter is a beautiful baby," the fairy agreed, "but, alas, she will never have any sense. She will be quite stupid."

The queen was most unhappy when she heard this, and when her second baby was born, she grew very unhappy. Her second daughter was very homely!

"Please don't cry," the good fairy said. "Your second daughter will be so clever and talented that no one will notice she is ugly."

"May Heaven grant your wish," sighed the queen. "But — is there no way that some of her good sense could be given to her sister?"

"I can do nothing to help your first daughter gain intelligence," the fairy answered. "But, because she is so lovely, I will give her a gift. She will be able to pass this beauty to anyone she deeply loves so that he, too, will be beautiful."

And so the two little princesses grew up. The first princess grew lovelier each day, and the second princess grew more intelligent. Everywhere people talked about the beautiful princess and her clever sister.

Visitors to the palace always crowded around the lovely sister first. She was so senseless she never knew what to say to them. Little by little, they would drift across the room to sit with the clever sister. She could talk and laugh for hours at a time. Nobody ever noticed how plain and ugly she was.

Sometimes the queen couldn't help scolding her stupid, lovely daughter. "You are so clumsy and senseless," she would say, "and you grow worse day by day!"

This always saddened the beautiful princess.

One day, when she was very sad, she walked deep into the forest. There, all alone, she sat down and cried. "How I wish I had brains instead of beauty," she wept.

A young man, dressed in rich and costly clothes, approached. As he came nearer, the princess was amazed at his awful ugliness. He was Prince Ricky-of-the-Tuft. He had been searching for the princess, for he had seen her picture and had fallen deeply in love with her. He could hardly believe his good luck in finding her here, alone in the forest.

"Your Highness," he greeted her in his most gracious manner. And then, seeing how sad she was, he asked, "Why are you so unhappy? Anyone as lovely as you should have no reason to weep. I have seen many beautiful women, but none of them as beautiful as you."

"You are very kind to say so, sir," replied the princess. "But I would much rather be as ugly as you are and intelligent than be beautiful and stupid!"

And she began to cry all over again.

"I can change that," said Ricky-of-the-Tuft. "I am able to give the gift of intelligence to the one I love the best and I love you! I can make you clever and talented and intelligent, if you will promise to marry me."

The princess was speechless with surprise. She didn't know what to say.

"You may have one year to make up your mind," Ricky-of-the-Tuft said kindly.

The poor little princess, without a brain in her head, had the silly idea that the year would never end. She was so anxious to be clever and witty that she cried out, "Yes, yes. I will marry you one year from today."

Right away, she was a different woman. Her conversation sparkled with charm and wit and she discussed affairs of state brilliantly.

"I think she is smarter than I am," Ricky thought to himself.

Her mother and father — and all the court — were amazed at this change in her. Young men came from far and near, asking her hand in marriage. But she was so much more clever than they were that she refused them all, one after another.

Then one day a very handsome prince came to call. He was so gallant, so rich, and so very brilliant that the princess thought she might marry him. She forgot all about her promise to Ricky-of-the-Tuft.

Trying to make up her mind about her marriage, she walked deep into the forest one day. It was the very same walk she had taken when she had met Prince Ricky. As she walked along, deep in thought, she heard a strange noise beneath her feet. It was a muffled, hurrying sound, as of people coming and going. "Pass me the saucepan," she heard someone say. Then, "Give me that chafing dish! Put more wood on the fire!"

Suddenly, the ground opened and, deep within the earth, she saw a huge kitchen. It was filled with cooks and scullery boys and all kinds of people, busily fixing a great feast.

"What are you doing?" asked the princess.

"Madam," replied the chief cook, "we are fixing the wedding feast of Prince Ricky-of-the-Tuft. He is to be married tomorrow."

And the princess gasped, suddenly remembering her promise to the ugly young prince. She had made the promise when she didn't have a brain in her head and had completely forgotten it when she had grown intelligent.

She had gone only a few steps when she met Ricky-of-the-Tuft.

"Ah, madam," he said, with a courtly bow. "It is exactly one year since you promised to marry me. Are you ready for our wedding tomorrow?"

"To be truthful, sir," the princess answered, "I still have not made up my mind. As you know, I could not make up my mind when I was dull and stupid. And now that you have given me so much intelligence, it is even harder for me to find someone who pleases me. You never should have taken away my stupidity."

"Princess," said the young prince, "do you find that I displease you?"

"No, no," cried the princess. "I am very pleased with everything about you — your ability, your disposition and your manner."

"But," said Ricky-of-the-Tuft, "I am very ugly."

"Yes," the princess sighed, "you are."

"If you love me," the prince said softly, "you can

change that. The same fairy who made it possible for me to give intelligence to the one I love, gave you the power to give beauty to your beloved."

And the lovely princess looked at the ugly young prince and said, "I wish, with all my heart, that you may become the most handsome and lovable prince in the world."

No sooner had she spoken than Ricky-of-the-Tuft became, in her eyes, the most handsome young prince on earth.

Some say it was the gift from the fairy — and some say it was because she looked at him with love. They were married the very next day.

The Son of the Baker
of Barra

Once a baker of Barra had a son and one son only, and the son's name was Ian Beg. There was nothing wrong with the lad at all, except that he was so goodhearted he'd give the coat off his back to anyone who wanted it, and follow it with his shirt if that was asked for too.

One day the baker of Barra made a very fine cake and told his son to take it up to the castle so that the king's daughter could have it for her supper.

"That I'll do and gladly," said Ian Beg. "Give me the cake, then, and let me be on my way." So the baker laid the cake in a clean white cloth, and gave it to his son.

It was a fair way to go to the castle, but the lad walked along briskly, carrying the cake by the corners of the cloth gathered into his hands. The road ran along by a stream, and then it ran along through the glen, and then it took a turn into a wood that stood in the way. There under the trees Ian Beg met three old gray *cailleachs*,[1] and he gave them *"Fáilte"* [2] and bade them leave him go by. But the three old women stood in his way and would not let him pass.

"Fáilte, Ian, son of the baker of Barra," they said. "What is in the napkin that you carry it with such care?"

" 'Tis a cake my father made for the daughter of the king," Ian answered proudly. "And 'tis myself that is taking it to her, that she may have it for her supper the night."

"For the king's daughter, do you say!" said the first old gray cailleach.

"Such a cake would be a wonder to see!" the second one said.

"Could you not open the napkin a wee bit and let us just have the smidgen of a look at it?" the third one begged.

Well, a bit of a look could do no harm, so Ian opened the napkin and showed them the cake.

[1] cailleachs — old women
[2] Fáilte — welcome

When he thought they had admired it long enough, he got ready to gather up the cloth about it so that he could be on his way again. But the three old caileachs would not let him.

"Not more than two or three times in my life have I tasted such a cake," said the first one.

"Not more than once in my life have I done the same," sighed the second one.

And then the third one said, "Och, I have ne'er once, in all the days of my life, put so much as a crumb of such a cake in my mouth!"

Then, as if the thought struck them all at the one time, they cried out, "Och, Ian Beg, *mo graidh*,[3] will ye not let us have a wee crumb to taste of the cake?"

Well, Ian being so goodhearted, although he wanted to say no, he could not do it. So he held the cake up on his hand, and told them they might each pinch off a wee crumb of it, but to make sure to take it where it wouldn't show.

And so they did. They savored the wee bit of a crumb with delight and Ian, pleased with their pleasure, forgot where his duty lay.

"Och, now, have a wee bit more," he pressed them kindly. " 'Twill ne'er be missed!" And to encourage them, he took a taste of the cake himself. Then one crumb followed another, and all of a sudden Ian Beg discovered the cloth was empty except

[3] mo graidh — my dear. This is what the Irish "machree" comes from.

105

for a few last crumbs. Among them all they'd finished the cake.

"Och," Ian Beg lamented. "Now the king's daughter will have no cake for her supper, and my father will flay the skin off my back when I go home."

"Och, nay, Ian Beg!" the first old cailleach told him. "Do you think so poorly of us to think we'd let you go home to face your father's wrath, and the three of us doing naught to save you?"

Then she took the cloth from his hand and folded it carefully to keep the crumbs inside. The three old creatures passed it from one to another until it came back to the hands of the first one again. She put it into the hands of Ian Beg. "Carry the napkin home to your father," she bade him. "Tell him to shake it out over the table and I'll warrant he'll be leaving the skin of your back alone. That will pay you for what I had of the cake. As for my sisters, they will pay for their share some time when you're needing it more than now."

"Tell your father to bake another cake for you to take to the king's daughter in the morn."

Ian Beg, being a biddable lad, did, as he was told. When he got home his father asked him, "Were they liking the cake at the castle?" for he was eager to keep the castle trade.

"They were not!" said Ian Beg. "And how would

they be liking it, the way they never got it?" he asked.

"Ne'er got it?" said the baker. "And why did they not?"

"Och, on the road through the wood I met three old gray cailleachs who begged so prettily for a taste of the cake that I let them have it," said Ian Beg. "And then they ate it all up."

"You let them have it!" roared the baker, reaching for his great wooden paddle that he put the loaves into the oven with. "Och, I'll be letting you have a bit of something too, my fine lad!"

"Not so fast," cried Ian Beg, skipping nimbly out of the way of the paddle. "Here's the cloth the cake was in, and they bade me tell you to shake the cloth out over the table, and you'd be willing to leave me be."

The baker grumbled, but he set the batter paddle aside. Taking the cloth in his hands he went over to the table, where he unfolded it and shook it out above the table top.

"Och! Crumbs!" he said, looking at them with disgust. "Losh! Have we not crumbs enough in our bakehouse now?" But before he had finished speaking every crumb had turned into a shining golden coin. "Look ye now, lad!" the baker cried joyfully. "Well paid am I for the cake, and no mistake. And a very good thing it was for you to let the old ones have the cake, for I'm thinking that they belong to the People of Peace, the fairy folk, themselves."

"I'd not be knowing about that," said Ian Beg. "They looked to me like any old cailleachs you might be meeting. But they said to tell you to bake another cake for me to take to the king's daughter in the morn."

As Ian Beg said, so it was done, and the next day Ian went off again with a cake for the king's daughter wrapped in a fresh white cloth which he carried with the four corners of it gathered into his hand. He went along by the stream, and then he went along through the glen, and into the wood and out of it again. This day he did not see the three old gray cailleachs at all, but when he came out of the wood and took the high road, he saw a great *sluagh*[4] of gentlefolk all on their way to the castle like himself. Some rode by on horseback and some rolled by in carriages, but he was the only one with naught but his own legs to carry him there. So he strode along in the dust of their passing, and soon he found himself trudging along behind them all. When he got to the castle he asked the man who guarded the door what was the occasion that had brought so many of the gentry there that day.

" 'Tis the birthday of the daughter of the king,"

4 sluagh — a lot, a great many

said the man. "And now that she is of an age to wed, she has given out the word that she will have for a husband the man who brings her the gift she likes the best."

" 'Tis nothing to me," said Ian Beg. "I am not in the running, for all I've brought is the cake that my father, the baker of Barra, made this morn for the supper of the daughter of the king."

So the man passed Ian Beg through the door, and Ian went into the castle hall with his cake.

The king sat in his chair of state at a long table, which was placed at one end of the hall. Beside him sat his daughter, ready to choose the gift that she preferred above all the rest. One by one, the gentlemen came up to the table and set their gifts upon it for her to see. Some gentlemen were very young, and some were very old, and the others were somewhere in between, but the lot of them all had the same proud and haughty look that showed they thought very well of themselves.

The richness of their gifts was beyond imagination, and soon the top of the table glimmered and glittered and shone with the gold and the silks and the precious stones that covered it from end to end. The king's daughter sat and looked down at the brave show with as little interest as if all these rich things were no more than pebbles and shells and driftwood, such as a child might find along the shore.

When the last gift had been laid on the table, and the suitors had drawn off to the side to wait until the choice was made, Ian Beg walked up, and pushing some of the gifts aside to make room for it, he set his cake down on the table in front of the daughter of the king.

" 'Tis no gift at all that I'm bringing you," he told her. "Naught but a cake that my father, the baker of Barra, made for your supper this night."

The king's daughter looked at the cake and then she looked at the lad who had brought it. Her eyes began to smile but as yet her lips did not. "*Moran taing*! [5] Thank you!" she said gravely. "Thank you, son of the baker of Barra, for the cake. It will come in handy, this being my birthday, and us without a crumb of cake in the house before you came."

Her eyes saw more than the cake, although that was well worth seeing. What she saw, was that the lad was tall and well-built, a big, handsome, yellow-haired laddie, and under the dust that had gathered upon him, stirred up by the wheels of the carriages and by the horses' feet, his face was bonny and good-humored, and she could tell that he was honest too. But she asked him to stand to the

[5] Moran taing — many thanks

side, for the moment, while she settled in her mind which of the gifts on the table she'd choose.

She looked the gifts over again, and then she looked at the suitors, and the more she saw of the latter the less she liked them. Slowly she rose from her chair beside the king, her father. The time had come for her to make her decision known. And so she did.

In a clear voice she said, "Jewels galore I have and more I need not. Silks I have in abundance — so many that I shall never wear them all. I am no longer a bairn[6] so I have no use for your golden toys and trinkets. The gift I like best is the cake that was brought to me by the son of the baker of Barra, and he's the one I shall wed!"

Ian Beg thought that his ears belied him, but the king's daughter looked at him, and her lips were smiling now, as well as her eyes.

"Will you have me then, son of the baker of Barra?" she asked him.

Ian's heart leaped within him for joy, and he answered. "Och, I don't mind if I do!"

Then there was a great to-do in the castle when the suitors understood that the king's daughter had passed them and their gifts by for a dusty baker's lad and a cake. They all seized their gifts in a great huff and went home. So there was the cake, sitting

[6] bairn — child

alone upon the table, with the king and his daughter behind it, and Ian Beg before.

"Well, my dear," said the king to his daughter, "I have naught to say against the baker of Barra. A very good baker he is, to be sure. And his son, no doubt, is a very fine lad. And this cake well may be, and probably is, the very best of cakes. But after all, a cake is a cake, and a husband is a husband. A cake is soon eaten and forgotten, and other cakes take its place. But a husband you must keep until the end of your days. Why not let the son of the baker of Barra go home to his father who will bake you a cake every day if you like?"

"Nay!" said his daughter. "My choice is made. I'll bide by it, come what may."

Och, this will not do at all! the king thought to himself. The world would ne'er stop laughing, should I let my daughter wed with a baker's son. He knew he'd never be able to argue his daughter out of it, for she was terribly set in her mind, and what she said she'd do, she intended to do. He sat looking at the pair of them; then he suddenly had what seemed to him a very good thought.

"Och, well," said the king to his daughter, "if you're of a mind to have the lad for a husband, I'll have naught to say against it. But you being my daughter, and my lone bairn, you'll understand I have your welfare at heart. No home have you e'er had in your life but in a castle, with all that was in it exactly as a king's daughter should have it. I have my doubts that you could be happy otherwise. You may wed the son of the baker of Barra with my blessing when he can give you a castle as good as this one, with everything in it the way you've always had it forbye. Now I've had my say, and 'tis all I'll say."

The king's daughter looked sadly at Ian Beg, but Ian Beg gave her a great smile. "A man can but try," he told her. "Will you wait for me till I come back again?" he asked.

"Aye!" replied the king's daughter. "I'll wait."

Then Ian Beg went home and told his father what the king had said.

"Now, bake me some bannocks[7] to eat on the road, and give me your blessing," said Ian Beg. "And I'll be off. The world will be my pillow and the sky will be my coverlet, and I'll find a castle for the king's daughter to live in or I'll not come back at all."

Ian Beg's father gave him a bundle of bannocks and his blessing and wished him Godspeed, and off Ian went on his journey. But though he traveled the length of the land, up and down and back and forth for many a weary mile, and saw many a strange sight upon the way, he could not find a castle for

[7] bannocks — oatcakes

himself. At last he came to the end of the world, and there was no place farther for him to go, for there was nothing before him but the great empty green sea with the gray sky beyond it.

"*Truagh mo charadh!* How heavy my sorrow!" said Ian Beg, and he stood and stared hopelessly at the sea. Then his eye caught a glimpse of a house that stood beyond on the shore, and as the night was drawing in and he was weary, he thought he would go there and ask for shelter until the day's dawn. So up to the house he went, and the door was open, so he went in. There were three seated there at the table, and he saw in the blink of an eye that it was the three old gray cailleachs whom he had met in the wood. They looked up at him as he came in and cried out a greeting.

"*Fáilte!* Welcome, Ian Beg," said the first one.

"*Mile fáilte!* A thousand welcomes!" the second one said.

"*Ceud mile fáilte!* A hundred thousand welcomes!" said the third. "Now that you're here, you must have a bite to eat with us."

So Ian Beg drew up a stool and sat down to the table. Then the old women discovered that he ate little, but sat leaning his head upon his hand, so they asked him how he came to be so sad. Soon they had coaxed all of Ian's troubles out of him, and himself was telling them everything that had happened to him since he last saw them in the wood.

"I've been up and down and back and forth through all the weary world, and there's not a castle that has not an owner to it already," Ian said.

"Och, I'd not say that," said the first old cailleach.

" 'Tis not impossible to find a castle," the second one said.

" 'Tis not, to be sure," said the third one. "Only you must choose the proper place to look."

"I'll give you a wee bit of something to help you," said the second old gray cailleach, and she took out of her sleeve a small, black iron box. The three old women passed it about among them from one to another until it came into the hands of the second one again.

"I've not forgotten your kindness in sharing the cake with us," said she, as she put the wee box in his hands. "This will pay for what I had of it, but be careful to keep it always with you, for it is a box that can do you good or harm!"

Ian Beg thanked her, and took the box and dropped it into his pouch, but indeed, he could not see how such a wee box could help him, so he soon forgot about it. But telling the old sisters about his troubles so relieved him that he felt as if a great load of grief had slipped off his back, and he slept very well that night.

In the morning they woke Ian Beg early and

started him off upon his way home, bidding him to be of good heart for he'd be finding his castle very soon. So back he went through the world, up hill and down and over moor and mountain, and on the third day he came to a stream in flood and the water was too deep for crossing, so he sat down to rest a bit and cool his feet in the stream before seeking a better place to get across. While he was sitting there a hunger came on him, for all that day he had not passed so much as a shepherd's bothan[8] where he could beg a bite to eat. As he felt around in his sporran[9] to find if a bit of bannock remained there, his fingers came upon the box that the second gray sister had given him, so he took it out. Och, what was the good of a wee iron box, and what would be in it, forbye?

So he opened the box.

Out jumped three spry lads, crying out *"Easgadh!*[10] Easgadh! Ready! Ready, Master Baker's Son!"* and bowing low before Ian Beg, they asked politely, "What will you have us do for you?"

When Ian Beg got over his surprise, he told them to bring him food at once. Soon they brought him his dinner on a great silver tray, and waited upon him while he ate. When he had finished he told

[8] bothan — a hut
[9] sporran — a pouch that is hung from the belt.
[10] Easgadh! — ready!

them that he needed nothing more, so into the box they popped. Ian shut the lid down upon them and put the box into his pouch again. "Och," said he, "if these creatures can bring me a dinner so easily, happen they can help me to a castle too." Then off he went on his journey again, lighthearted and fast-footed, and within a few days, reached home.

The baker of Barra was happy to have his son back again. As for the castle, the baker was of the opinion that Ian was well enough off without it, and as for the king's daughter, who ever heard of one of those who wedded a baker's son?

Ian said naught one way or the other to all his father told him. He said not a word about the wee iron box either, but ate his supper and went early to bed.

While the moon was yet high and the night dark and still, Ian rose from his bed and got into his clothes. Out of the house he went, and down the road, along by the stream and through the glen, until he came to the wood. There he took out the wee box and opened it, and at once the three spry lads leaped out, crying "Easgadh! Easgadh! Master Son of the Baker! What will you have us do for you?"

"Build me a fine castle here, with the wood to be a park about it, and the castle to be bigger than the king's own and better. Make everything in it finer than anything in the king's house, and put a great stable behind it, and in the stable a gold coach with four white horses to draw it for me to go to the king's castle in, in the morn. And look to it that there be plenty of servants, both indoors and out, that the king's daughter and myself may be well served."

Long before cock's crow that morn all was done, exactly as Ian had commanded. The three spry lads were back in their box, and box safely in Ian's pouch again.

When the sun was high in the sky that morn, Ian Beg dressed in his best and rode up to the king's castle in his gold coach drawn by white horses with gold plumes on their heads. There was a fine coachman to drive the horses, with four footmen behind, and a postilion riding before. The king looked out the window and wondered who this grand laird [11] was that came riding so fine. His daughter came and looked over his shoulder, and then she laughed aloud.

"Och, what way would your eyes be telling you 'tis a laird at all?" she asked. "Is it not plain to be seen that 'tis Ian Beg, come back to make me his bride?"

The king was terrible vexed. "Och, well," he grumbled, "happen the lad has got hold of a coach

[11] laird — lord, or nobleman

and four horses, but that does not mean he'll be having the castle too."

"Aye, but he will!" the king's daughter said.

After the king saw Ian's castle, he could say no more against the wedding of his daughter to the baker's son. Had not the lad got a castle even bigger and better than his own? So the wedding was set for a week come Sunday, and the king's daughter hurried off to see to her wedding gown, while Ian Beg took his gold coach back to his castle and left it there. Then he walked home to his father's house and there wasn't a man in Barra that day could match him for happiness.

He was late getting to bed that night, because he had so much to tell his father, and it took time to make the baker understand that his baking days were over, and that he should sell his bakehouse and live at ease for the rest of his days. It wasn't until he was getting ready for bed that Ian discovered that his wee iron box was not in his pouch.

"Och, woe!" he said, yawning. "I've laid it down somewhere up at the castle, no doubt. Well, I'm too tired to go fetch it now. I'll rise early and go for it, in the morn." Half asleep, he tumbled into bed.

When the king came home from having a look at Ian Beg's castle, he sat and chewed his fingers with rage. There was some trick or other about the way Ian Beg's castle had appeared, but what it was he couldn't think. At least, he decided, he could see the spae-wife[12] and see what she could tell him. She had the name for having all sorts of uncanny wisdom, and folk called her a witch. Maybe she could tell him what to do.

So down the stairs he stomped, and out the back door of the castle and kept on going until he came to the spae-wife's cottage at the end of the hen run. The spae-wife cast her spells for him and then she said. "It has all been done with the help of a magic box that the People of Peace have given the baker's son. As long as he carried it with him there was nothing you could do about it, but by mischance he has mislaid it this night. You will find it where it has slipped down behind the cushions of his gold coach. My advice to you is take your daughter at once to the castle, and when you have found the box tell those who come out of it when you open it to take the castle, yourself, and your daughter to some distant place where the son of the baker will not be able to find you."

"Well and good," said the king. "But where would such a place be?"

"The Island of the Kingdom of the Rats would be the best place," the spae-wife said. "I doubt he'll e'er have heard tell of it. You should be safe there."

The king did as the spae-wife told him. He went

[12] spae-wife — a witch, a wise woman

back to his castle and roused his daughter from her bed, and made her go to Ian's castle with him that very night. Long before Ian Beg woke in the morning the three spry lads from the wee black box had obeyed the king's command and carried the king and the king's daughter and the castle of Ian Beg to the Island of the Kingdom of the Rats far away over the sea, and set them all down there.

When Ian Beg went up the road to his castle in the morning his heart was blithe and gay, but when he got to the wood, it sank like a weight of lead. There was no sign of a castle among the trees, and all that was left was the bare empty space where it had stood.

Ian rushed up to the king's castle to tell the king's daughter that his castle was gone, but neither the king nor his daughter were at home, the servants said. All that they could say was that the king had taken his daughter and gone away with her in the night, and where he had taken her they would not be able to say, for they had not been told. So Ian Beg went back to the wood and sat down by the road, not knowing what else to do. While he was sitting there, along the road the three old cailleachs came, and stopped before him.

"Och, Ian Beg! What is the trouble now?" they said.

Ian Beg looked up at them and answered. "Och,

my castle is gone, and the king's daughter, and my wee black box as well."

"You should have kept the wee box with you," said the second old cailleach. "We knew by our spells that it was gone. 'Tis why we came."

"The king got hold of the box and used it to carry the castle and his daughter away," her sisters said.

"How could I be knowing he'd do the like? I'd not have thought it of a king!" said Ian Beg. "Och, well, 'tis my own fault for being careless. The castle's gone and the lass is gone, and without the box I cannot get them back again, so there's naught I can do about it. I'll go back to my father and help him in the bakehouse."

"Och, do not talk so daft!" said the third old cailleach. "You must go after them and bring the lot of them home."

"What luck would I have at that," asked Ian Beg, "and me not even knowing where they've gone?"

"That we can tell you," said the old cailleachs. "It's over the sea to the Island of the Kingdom of the Rats the castle and the king and his daughter have gone."

"In that case it might as well be behind the world's end for all that I can do," said Ian Beg.

"You're forgetting one thing," the third old cailleach told him. "Am I not here to help you, and me still beholden to you for my share of your cake?" So she took Ian Beg by the hand and pulled him up to his feet, and led him away until they came to the shore of the sea.

"You'll be needing a ship," she said. And looking about her, she picked up a piece of driftwood that lay nearby on the sands. She tossed it out upon the waves and at once it became a fine ship.

"Now you'll be needing a captain to chart your course and steer your ship," she said. She looked about her again and saw a great black cat on the shore catching a fish for his supper, so she picked him up and threw him upon the deck of the ship.

"You shall be captain," she told the cat, "and sail the ship."

So the cat sat up straight in the captain's place, waiting the word to go.

"Now heed me well, Ian Beg," said the third old gray cailleach. "When you get to the Island of the Kingdom of the Rats, do not set foot from the ship, but send the cat to get the box and bring it to you. And when you have it safe in your hands again, you will know what to do."

Then Ian Beg thanked her for her help, and bade her farewell, and joined the cat on the ship. The cat sailed the ship well, and in good time they came to the place in the sea where the Island of the King-dom of the Rats lay, and there Ian Beg saw his cas-tle rising up high and proud a short piece up from

the shore. The cat brought the ship up to a wharf of stones and anchored it, and Ian was just about to step off the ship, when he remembered what the old cailleach had said. So he told the cat to go up to the castle and find his wee black iron box and bring it back to him.

The cat jumped out of the ship, and the first thing he saw was a huge rat sitting at the end of the wharf, fishing with its tail for a line. The cat, being hungry, pounced on the rat and held him down, intending to have him for his supper.

"Nay!" said the rat, trembling with fear from his whiskers to the tip of his tail. "Pray do not eat me! Spare my life and I will help you. I know this kingdom better than you will ever know it, and if there is anything I can get for you I will gladly do so."

The cat held the rat down while he thought the offer over. At last he said, "It's a wee black iron box I'm wanting, and from what I hear it's somewhere in that castle up there. Have you seen it anywhere about?"

"That I have!" cried the rat. "As I came by the castle not long ago, such a box lay on one of the window sills near the road. Let me go and I'll fetch it for you."

So the cat released the rat and away he ran. Soon the rat came back with the box and gave it to the cat, who carried it to Ian Beg. Ian Beg opened the

box and out jumped the three spry lads crying,
"Easgadh! Easgadh! Ready! Ready! What will you
have us do for you?" And Ian Beg wasted no time in
telling them what to do.

"Carry my castle back to the place in the wood
where it belongs, with the king's daughter and the
king in it too," he told them. "And let one of you
make sure to beat the king well, all the way back,
for making you bring my castle here."

So the three spry lads jumped off the ship and the
cat jumped on, and the cat sailed the ship back
home.

When they got back to Barra, Ian Beg got off the
ship and started out to walk back to the wood in
which he had built his castle. The cat got off the
ship too, and went to catch a fish for his supper —
and what became of the ship nobody knows. Ian
walked up the road along by the stream, and
through the glen, and came at last to the wood, and
there was his castle, standing tall and proud among
the trees again.

In front of the castle were the three old cailleachs
and the three spry lads, and the king, who was looking a bit battered and dazed from the beating he'd
got for taking the castle away. And, best of all, there
was the king's daughter herself, running to meet
him and to welcome him home.

So the king's daughter married the son of the

baker of Barra, and a very grand wedding it was. The king kept his promise and gave the young couple his blessing. He could not do less, for he knew that his son-in-law had in his pouch the wee black iron box that had the three spry lads within it, and the king had no wish to make their acquaintance again.

The wedding lasted for a week and a month and a day, and the guests came from far and near. There were so many guests at the wedding that both the king's castle and Ian Beg's were filled with folk. And who came to the wedding but the three old cailleachs, and they sat at the table with Ian Beg, who showed them every kind attention he could. There was music and dancing and feasting from morn till morn, and, for those who wanted to hear them, there were tellers of tales and those with such stories as you ne'er heard before. It was from one of them that I got this story that I've just told you about the son of the baker of Barra who married the king's daughter, and the two of them lived happily in Ian Beg's castle all the rest of their days.